QUEEN BEE

QUEEN BEE

a novel by

Mark Anthony

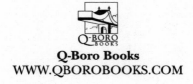

Q-Boro Books
WWW.QBOROBOOKS.COM

An Urban Entertainment Company

ISBN-13: 978-1-933967-89-9
ISBN-10: 1-933967-89-7
LCCN: 2008921267

First Printing November 2008
Printed in the United States of America

10 9 8 7 6 5 4

Cover Copyright © 2008 by Q-BORO BOOKS, all rights reserved.
Cover layout/design: Candace K. Cottrell; Photo: Frank Antonio;
Model: Sasha
Editors: Brian Sandy, Candace K. Cottrell

Q-BORO BOOKS
Jamaica, Queens NY 11434
WWW.QBOROBOOKS.COM

Chapter One

Brazil

"Hey, sweetie, where's your mommy? Is she home?"
"Yeah, she's in the back doing her hair. Wait here.
I'll go get her. Mommy! Mommy! Auntie Essence is here to
see you."

I could hear my daughter yelling to get my attention as
I stood in front of my mirror blow-drying my hair. I had
just finished polishing my toenails when Angie, my six-
year-old daughter, came bursting into my bedroom like
she'd lost her mind. She didn't even realize that she had
accidentally knocked over my red nail polish.

"Angie, what the fuck is wrong wit'chu? Watch where
you going! You got nail polish all over my floor now."

"I'm sorry, Mommy. I was just coming to tell you that
Auntie Essence is here," my daughter said as she stood in
her tracks breathing heavy from running.

I turned off the blow-dryer and placed it on my dresser.
With cotton balls between my toes I walked toward the
front door of the two-family house that I was renting in
the Rosedale section of Queens, New York. I was wearing
pink lace boy shorts that barely covered my ass and I had

on a tight white wife-beater with no bra underneath, which accentuated my double D breasts.

"Oh, Essence, I thought you was by yourself. Let me go throw on my robe," I said to Essence, who was standing in the foyer near my front door with her man, Tut. Everyone on the street referred to him as King Tut. "Hey, Tut," I added before turning to go get my robe.

Although I didn't feel uncomfortable with what I was wearing, I knew how Essence was, so I knew it would be best if I went and put on my robe. Essence was the type who would be cursing me out the next day for *trying to show off my body to her man*, or for *trying to entice her man*. She was as gorgeous as they come, but at the same time she was definitely the insecure and insanely jealous type.

"Nah, Brazil, fuck the robe. We gotta talk. We got a problem," Essence said with an attitude that I was all too familiar with.

King Tut and Essence made their way into my living room, and I quickly scanned through my mind trying to recall any events or anything that might have involved me fucking up in some way. The first thing that I thought of was that maybe Essence had got hip to the fact that I had been stealing money from her. But I was always on point and I always kept things thorough, so I knew that, whatever it was, it more than likely didn't involve me directly.

"What's up? What happened?" I said as a drop of water fell from my naturally straight jet-black hair and on to my shoulder.

"What happened is, we got a problem. And the problem is that you a muthafuckin' snitch!" Essence said to me as she approached me. "I told you about running your mouth."

"What are you talking about?"

"Brazil, you know exactly what I'm talking about. I

don't got time for no bullshit," Essence barked in my face as some of her spit landed on my cheek. The spit instantly caused me to lose my temper and I tried my hardest to hold everything in check but I wasn't gonna let her disrespect me, especially not in my own house, regardless if she was my boss.

"Hol' up, Essence. Back up off of me, or we gonna have a problem for real, for real!"

Essence didn't respond with words, but she did respond with a right hook that landed on my jaw and caused me to stumble. The blow caught me off guard because Essence had always been the type to talk a lot of shit and intimidate people with her mouth, but I had never seen her actually use her hands.

Although Essence was taller than me, I had more meat on my body than she did, so I knew that I was stronger than her. I immediately grabbed her by her shirt with both of my hands and forced her backwards and rammed her into my living room wall. The force was so strong that her body literally put a huge hole in the sheet rock. Picture frames and my flat-screen TV that was on the wall came crashing to the floor. With the wind knocked out of her, I proceeded to whip her ass.

My daughter came running into the living room to see what all of the commotion was about. Just as she entered the room, King Tut, who stood about six foot four and weighed 240 pounds of prison yard muscle, grabbed a fistful of my hair and forcefully yanked my 5-foot 4-inch body to the floor. I winced in pain as my daughter ran to my side.

"Mommy!"

"Angie, go to your room," I screamed at my daughter just as Essence ran up on me and started stomping me in my head with her stilettos. I knew that I had to quickly get to my feet, or else I was gonna get my ass beat.

"Angie, go to your room right now!" I hollered at my daughter, who ran off to her room crying in fear.

"Tut, hold this bitch down," Essence ordered.

King Tut forced me back to the floor and put his knee across my chest, pinning me down.

"Who the fuck you swinging on?" Essence shouted at me as she reached in her bag, pulled out a chrome revolver and aimed it at me.

My eyes got as wide as the hole that Essence's body had just put in my living room wall. I stopped dead in my tracks and stared down the barrel of her gun. "Wait, wait, wait, wait." I held my hands up in surrender while lying on my back.

"Nah, fuck that." Essence cocked her gun.

"What did I do?" I yelled. If I was gonna die I at least wanted to know what I was getting murdered for. My heart was racing a mile a minute, and my heavy breathing was restricted by Tut's knee pressing down on my chest.

"You know what the fuck you did. What the hell did you say to the cops the other night when they raided the club?"

"I ain't say shit," I quickly responded. "What are they saying?" I really got nervous at that point because I knew how cops lie and how they rely on confidential informants who lie and feed them bad information.

"Essence, she bullshitting. We ain't come here to play no games!" King Tut shouted. "You saw the affidavit. Kill this bitch. She a liability."

"Essence, I swear on the life of my daughter I ain't say shit," I continued to plead.

"Brazil, I saw your signature on an affidavit! Now explain that," Essence yelled.

King Tut got up from off of me, and I struggled to stand to my feet.

"Give me the ratchet," Tut ordered.

"Nah, I got this, babe," Essence responded. "Brazil, you can either see it coming, or you can turn the fuck around and take this bullet in the back of your head. Tell me how you wanna do this," Essence said to me.

From the look on her face and from the sound of her voice I could tell that she was serious.

"Yo, Essence, I'm telling you I ain't no snitch. You know me, Essence. We been homegirls from day one. I would never snake you like that."

Essence, in her high-heel shoes and her skintight Citizens of Humanity jeans, tightly gripped her gun, which was still aimed at my head. "From the front or from the back, tell me how you want it."

Almost on cue, my daughter came running into the living room and grabbed hold of my leg. She was still crying from earlier.

"Baby, just go to your room. Everything's okay," I feverishly said.

She looked at me and looked around the room before hesitantly strolling back off to her room.

"Essence, don't kill me here in front of my daughter. Do what you gotta do, but just not here." My stomach started to feel queasy as I was becoming resigned to my fate.

Essence looked at me, and then she looked at Tut.

"If we kill her, we gotta kill the kid too," Tut said.

"She's a baby! No please. Okay, okay, look, Essence, however you wanna do this, just do it, but please don't hurt my daughter. She's innocent. Kill me, but leave her alone."

"Essence, the kid can ID us," Tut replied.

"Brazil, get on your knees," Essence ordered.

My heavy breathing was clearly visible, and I felt like I was about to crap in my pants. I knew that I was about to die. I just didn't want my daughter to see me lying dead in a pool of blood, but at the same time, I more so didn't want her to be harmed in any way.

"Get the fuck on your knees now!"

I dropped to my knees, and although I was scared as hell I refused to let Essence get the satisfaction of having me continue to beg. I kept silent and stared her in her face, to test the "gangstress" in her.

"Open your mouth."

I stared into Essence's eyes, almost daring her to kill me. I was nervous and hoping that she didn't have the heart to go through with it. I opened my mouth and stared at her as she placed the steel barrel in my mouth and cocked it.

"You like running your mouth, right?" Essence sarcastically asked me.

I didn't flinch, but my eyes were burning a hole into Essence's eyes. I was too afraid to breathe.

Essence then took the gun from out of my mouth and whacked me across the head with it. I gasped from the pain and I spun and fell face first to the floor. Immediately I felt warm blood running down the right side of my caramel-colored face.

"I ain't gonna kill your sorry ass in front of your daughter, but word is bond, your ass is dying, fuckin' snitch-ass bitch!" Essence kicked me in the ribs and stormed out the house, and King Tut followed her out my front door.

I could hear her stilettos click-clacking in the background as I exhaled in relief.

Chapter Two

Destiny

It had been about five minutes or so since King Tut had left my apartment and my pussy was still jumping with sexual excitement from the good bareback dick that he had just given me. Tut had been secretly fucking me a few times a week ever since he'd come home from jail six months ago, and I loved every fuck session that we had.

I stood in my oversized T-shirt and rested both of my elbows on the railing of my balcony and took some pulls from the weed I was smoking. I sipped on my glass of Nutcracker liqueur. I was trying to hold back from calling Tut so soon after he'd left, but I didn't care, I had to speak to him. I gave in to my urges and called his cell phone.

"What's up, ma?" Tut said as he answered his cell phone. I could tell that he had a smile on his face.

"I'm busted, right?" I asked.

"Whatchu mean?"

"You know what I mean. I'm busted for catching feelings," I answered with a small amount of seriousness in my voice. "You know I'm on your dick. It's obvious."

Tut just chuckled into the phone, but he didn't verbally respond.

"Oh now you laughing at me?"

"Nah, nah, it's not that. I'm just saying, this shit is kinda crazy the way things just popped off between me and you."

"Yeah, it is. It's real crazy, but I love it though. So where you at?"

"I just made it to the bridge. I'm getting ready to pay this toll."

"Well, pay the toll and turn back around. I ain't want you to leave so soon. My pussy is still jumping," I said, hoping that Tut would take me up on my offer.

Tut explained that he didn't want to leave me so soon but that he had to hurry up and get over to the club and hold everything down for the night.

No sooner than he'd said that, my cell phone was ringing. It was Brazil on the other line.

"Tut, that's my other line. Let me go, I'll see you tonight." I hung up on Tut and took Brazil's call.

Immediately, I could tell that something was up with Brazil, just based on how loud she was talking. She was practically yelling into the phone as she spoke to me.

"Destiny, I swear to God, I'm either gonna be dead, or I'm going to jail tonight!"

"Why? What happened?"

"Essence and Tut, both of they asses is dying tonight! You better believe that shit. They ran up in my crib and had me on my knees with a gun jammed in my mouth. Right in front of my daughter," Brazil explained, shouting every word into the receiver.

"Get outta here. For what? When did this happen?"

"It happened about three hours ago. And over some bullshit. She claims that I snitched on her that night when the cops raided Promiscuous Girl. But you know and I know that this is just about Essence still being on that insecure, jealous shit. Ever since we told her that we was looking to open our own club she been acting funny. Matter of fact, ever since I got my Range Rover she started changing, acting all shady."

Brazil went on to run down exactly what had transpired earlier in the day between her, Essence, and Tut. I believed what she was saying because she had no reason to lie to me. What I couldn't understand was how Tut could come by my crib, sex my brains out, and leave, yet he never mentioned that him and Essence had confronted Brazil earlier in the day. It made me feel like Tut was just looking at me as if I was a ho or something, and meanwhile here I was catching feelings for the nigga.

It also made me think that if he could have just threatened Brazil's life one minute and sex me the next, then he was capable of switching up sides on me as well, so I knew I needed to be smart and be more careful with him.

I continued to listen to Brazil, but I didn't mention the fact that Tut had just left my crib. Although Brazil was my girl, I didn't even want her to know what was really good between me and Tut. I couldn't risk word getting back to Essence about me and Tut because I didn't need the drama. And not only that, but the majority of the money that I was getting was coming through Essence. Yes, I was fucking her man, but she was still the hand that was feeding me, and I couldn't mess that up. Not just yet anyway.

"Destiny, where you at right now?" Brazil asked me.

"I'm still in the crib. I'm gonna jump in the shower in a few and get dressed and head over to the club. Zab Judah, Young Jeezy, and some other celebrities are supposed to be coming through the spot tonight, so it's gonna be packed in there, and I wanna get there on time."

"A'ight, listen. This is what I wanna do. I just spoke to Vegas and he told me that he didn't want me and Angie staying in the house tonight 'cause he didn't want to risk

Essence coming back to the house and doing me or Angie
any harm. He ain't in town and he won't be back until tomorrow, so he told me to just chill and lay low until he
gets back. So what I wanna do is come by with Angie, let
us spend the night at your spot until the morning. Then I'll
take Angie to school in the morning, and then when Vegas
gets here I'll bounce," Brazil explained.

Brazil was my girl, so I didn't have a problem with her
or her daughter spending the night at my house. We had
met at Sue's Rendezvous strip club five years ago when
we both worked there as dancers. That was also where
we'd met Essence. Essence had come to Sue's Rendezvous
to recruit strippers for the new strip club that she'd opened
up called Promiscuous Girl. And since she was offering me
and Brazil a guaranteed weekly salary, in addition to the
money we were to make in tips, we both jumped at her
offer, and we've been with her at Promiscuous Girl for the
past three years.

In that three-year time frame, me and Brazil had gotten
pretty close, and to keep it totally real, it was me and
Brazil who had masterminded and started the prostitution
hustle at Promiscuous Girl. That was really why the club
became the number one strip club in New York and had
the best reputation among all of the celebrities.

See, Brazil had Brazilian roots, and she was able to recruit a bunch of bad-ass chicks from her country who
barely spoke any English but who were willing to come to
New York and work at Promiscuous Girl as strippers. And
when the girls got to New York and started working and were
pretty much dependent on her, that was when she would
give them the ultimatum of them also having to prostitute
themselves or risk getting their asses sent back to their
country with all loss of hope of ever becoming a United
States citizen. And since most of the chicks were already
prostituting themselves for a living in their country, it

wasn't hard at all for them to get on board with the program at Promiscuous Girl.

Essence got all the shine from being the owner of the club, but truth be told, it was me and Brazil who were the brains behind making that club really pop. So Essence really had no choice but to elevate me and Brazil to managers of the club. But, at the same time, she hated our ambition because she looked at it as a threat.

Vegas was Angie's father and a low-level hustler who was always in and out of town trying to make moves. Although he was getting a little money, if you let him tell it, he was running shit and getting money like John Gotti.

Brazil explained to me that when she told Vegas what had happened to her earlier that day that he was heated. Technically Vegas and Brazil were no longer seeing each other, even though they were still fucking each other. But what had pissed Vegas off so much was that Essence and Tut had shown total disrespect to Brazil in front of his daughter.

"Destiny, I already told Vegas to be ready to handle his business tomorrow. There ain't gonna be no talking and a bunch of back-and-forth shit."

I continued to talk to Brazil for a few more minutes, but I had to let her go. It was a little past nine o'clock, and I wanted to hurry up and get dressed so I could bounce. "A'ight, so listen. Hurry up and come through. I'm gonna start getting ready to go."

"Okay, we on our way. And, listen, when you speak to Tut or to Essence and if they checking for me, just tell them you ain't see me or hear from me."

"A'ight, no doubt," I said as I pressed the end button on my cell phone.

Chapter Three

Essence

Destiny thought she was playing me for a dummy by fucking King Tut behind my back. But, see, what she didn't know was that I was the one who orchestrated the whole thing between her and King Tut. I wanted to test her loyalty to me. And she failed the test big time.

There are basic rules to the game that shouldn't be broken, and whenever you get sloppy and start breaking them, you're just setting yourself up for a downfall. At the top of my list of rules: no stealing. I can't tolerate the shit 'cause if I had people around me who will steal from me, it would be just a matter of time before they'd hurt me in a far worse way.

Another one of the rules that shouldn't be broken: Never kill innocent kids over adult beef. So regardless of what Tut was telling me I should have done when we went to check Brazil, I knew that killing her daughter would have only led to my downfall.

And right at the top of my list of unbreakable rules, right next to "No snitching" was: Never fuck your friend's significant other.

Break any of those rules and it'll be the start of your downfall. That was just the honorable code that I'd always lived by, and so far my ghetto-fabulous life had been lovely as a result of my integrity.

I ran my Promiscuous Girl empire a certain way, and I know that I was perceived as this controlling, insecure diva. Yes, I liked to shine, I loved getting money and all of that just like everybody else, but the thing that I was biggest on was loyalty and honor. And when people were disloyal and had no honor and they ended up getting screwed or killed in the process, then that's just how it went. And that's on them, not on me.

As for Brazil and Destiny, they both knew that they'd broken the rules, but what they didn't know was that I was smart enough to know that. So it was only right that I screwed them for trying to screw me.

To me what was so sad was that me, Destiny, and Brazil, at one point, had developed a bond that was so close that we felt like sisters. And it was a shame to see that bond breaking and things starting to deteriorate like it was beginning to do. We were always on the same vibe, and our styles were similar. We liked the same shit, we fucked the same type of niggas. And when we weren't working, we hung out at the same spots. We even spoke alike and sounded like each other. It got to the point where if you were to blindfold someone and then have the three of us talk to that person, the person more than likely would have no idea if it was me, Destiny, or Brazil who was doing the talking. But like I said, unfortunately because of their trifling ways, that bond was quickly shattering into pieces.

Brazil had been stealing money from me on a regular basis and I knew that it was with that stolen money that she was planning on opening up a new strip club with Destiny as her partner. Even though I played blind to the fact that she'd been stealing from me, there was no way that I could stand around and let her open up a new club on my watch and on my dime. From the outside looking in, it would seem like I was hating on her come-up, but the reality was, she was trying to make her come-up with my dough that she'd stolen!

Brazil had masterminded this prostitution ring and it was bringing in a hell of a lot of money. I guess she thought that since she'd masterminded the whole thing she was entitled to skim money off the top. But shit didn't work like that.

The way the prostitution ring worked was like this: If a dude ordered a bottle of either Alizé or Hpnotiq from me, Brazil, or Destiny, we knew it was really just a disguise to pay for some pussy or for a blow job. For a bottle of Alizé we would charge dudes $150, and for a bottle of Hpnotiq we would charge $300. When we delivered the bottle to the dudes, they would point out one of the Brazilian dancers they wanted to get with, and we would arrange to make it happen.

To protect ourselves, we would never let anything go down sexually at the strip club. Instead, a cab would take the strippers to this motel near Kennedy Airport, which was about ten or fifteen minutes away from the strip club. And the guy who had paid for the blow job or for sex would meet up with the chick at the motel and get everything poppin' over there, far from our establishment, and with no money changing hands between him and the girl.

The girls were always safe because we would have a bodyguard on post at the motel to protect them. They would wait out in front or in the lobby with the bodyguard until the dude who'd paid for the sex arrived.

The operation worked perfectly and easily brought in ten grand and better on a good night. And since we were barely paying the hoes any of the money, most of that

money was pure profit. I guess it was just too much money
and too tempting for Brazil not to steal. I had set her up by
having more than twenty different guys order bottles of
Hpnotiq from her on numerous occasions. Then I just had
to do the math. Whenever she handed in her cash to me at
the end of the night she was always way short with her
dough. If she was supposed to give me two thousand, she
would give me twelve hundred. But I never said anything
or accused her of coming up short. I always just played
shit real cool while I watched her ass and plotted my plan.

Destiny had been consistently fucking King Tut for the
past six months and every day she saw me she would
smile in my face and talk all pleasant with me, like everything was all good. But it was cool, 'cause, see, I know
that a nigga can control any woman that he's sexing. And
I also I know that all women let their emotions get caught
up in the dick, even if it's supposed to just be about the
dick and nothing more. And I'd purposely wanted to be
able to fully control Destiny, yet I knew she would never
be smart enough to realize that I was controlling her
through my man's dick.

I loved Tut to no end, but at the same time I was realis-
tic. I knew that all dudes get pussy on the side, so the way
I looked at it, by me allowing and encouraging him to sex
Destiny for my benefit, it was helping to keep him happy
from a man's point of view, while at the same time it was
accomplishing what I needed accomplished. As long as
Tut didn't tongue-kiss her, eat her out, or anything inti-
mate like that, and as long as he used condoms whenever
he sexed her, I was good with the setup.

So what choices did I have, other than to get back at
the two chicks who were supposed to be my right-hand
girls? I had no other choice but to get back at them, but I
knew that I had to be smart about how I did it.

By the time Destiny arrived at the strip club, it wasn't fully packed but it was starting to get packed. The music was blasting, and I had already done about four lines of coke, so I was feeling real good.

"Look at you and your sexy ass," I said to her, admiring a Roberto Cavalli outfit and heels I'd never seen her in before. Destiny was a pretty girl. In fact, she was the spitting image of the singer Alicia Keys. Only, her body was a lot more voluptuous than Alicia Keys and she was a whole lot more ghetto. She had the old Mary J. Blige attitude and demeanor, but the modern-day Alicia Keys look. Destiny was twenty-three years old, had a big ass, big tits, nice legs. She was light-skinned with tattoos in all the right places, and drop-dead gorgeous in the face. To most guys, if not all, she had the total package and she was kid-free.

"*Mwah, mwah.*" Destiny exaggerated the kissing sound while she kissed me on both of my cheeks as she greeted me. "I'm just trying to be fly like you, that's all."

I smiled at her and continued to look at her outfit.

"It's gonna be on up in here tonight," Destiny said, stressing the word *tonight*.

"No question. Yo, listen, before it gets too crazy in here, I gotta talk to you about something really serious, but we gotta talk in private. I don't want nobody hearing what we saying."

Destiny told me that she would meet me in my office in a few minutes. She first wanted to say what's up to a few people, get a drink, and then she would be right there to see me. So in the interim I went and found Tut and had him come to my office, because in actuality I wanted him to do the talking for me. I had already filled him in on what I wanted him to speak to Destiny about.

After about fifteen minutes or so, Destiny came into my office and closed the door behind her, to try and drown out the sound of the loud music coming from inside the club. My office was decorated with a large desk and a plush burgundy leather executive chair and a matching leather sofa. It had a huge saltwater fish tank with all kinds of exotic fish inside of it, and just to the right of the fish tank was a huge flat-screen television that hung from the wall.

As I sat behind my desk I had a small sterling silver tray in front of me that had cocaine on it. I lifted up the tray and extended it in Destiny's direction, as if I were offering her hors d'oeuvres or something. "You want some of this?" I asked.

Destiny walked closer to my desk and shook her head no.

"You sure?" I asked sounding surprised. I had never known Destiny to turn down weed or coke or liquor.

"Yeah, I'm good," she replied.

I could tell that her wheels were turning and that she was trying hard to figure out what was up.

Tut was sitting on the couch with a poker face. I purposely kept quiet in order to make Destiny feel uneasy and I slowly snorted a line of coke. I waited a few seconds and then I lifted my head from the tray. I smiled. "I'm loving those shoes," I said to Destiny. "Roberto Cavalli, right?"

"Yeah, Roberto Cavalli."

Everyone who came into my office, except for Tut, knew that they were subject to my rule of not being able to sit down unless I asked them to have a seat.

"You want me sit?" Destiny asked, showing me the utmost respect at that point.

I couldn't help but smirk as I thought to myself, *Phony-ass bitch, a few hours ago you was fucking my man.* "Yeah, definitely. Have a seat on the couch. We got a serious issue that we gotta handle," I told her.

Destiny looked at Tut but didn't say anything. She seemed to be trying to read his mind, and then she sat down.

"When was the last time you spoke to Brazil?" I asked her.

"Last night right before I left the club. Why? What's going on?"

Tut stepped in and answered, "What's going on is that Brazil is trying to get all of us locked up."

Destiny looked at me confused.

"Destiny, I'ma be straight up with you. I know you and Brazil are getting ready to open up that new spot, and that's all good and I'm happy for y'all. It's enough money out here for all of us to eat," I explained.

Destiny nodded her head in agreement.

"But Brazil is looking out for Brazil, and that's it. What she's trying to do is get all of us knocked so that she can open up that spot and not have to worry about competing against Promiscuous Girl or splitting money with you as her partner." I lifted my glass of Hennessy on the rocks and took a swig.

"I'm lost," Destiny replied.

Tut handed Destiny a copy of an affidavit that had Brazil's signature on it and told her to read it.

As Destiny read the four-page document, I explained to her, "And when you finish reading it, look at that signature and you'll see that it has Brazil's government name on it. And it's an original signature. That shit ain't no photo-copy."

"Wow! This is breaking down everything," Destiny replied.

"Exactly! She broke down the whole prostitution oper-ation and all that. That shit right there that you holding in your hands is gonna get all of our asses indicted, you watch!" I stressed to her. "And she got *your* muthafuckin' name all up in that shit more than my name."

"But how you know this shit is real? Did you speak to her?"

"How do I know the shit is real?" I said in disbelief. I

pushed my chair away from my desk and stood up. "Destiny, she signed the shit. That's her handwriting. I can go show you just regular everyday invoices and shit like that she's signed for in the past and you'll be able to see that it's the exact same signature."

Destiny asked me, "Well, how did y'all get a copy of the affidavit so soon? And an original copy at that?"

I walked from behind my desk. I shook my head and smiled. "Destiny, you trying to give me a complex or something? What the fuck? You wanna go to jail or what?"

"Essence, no disrespect, I'm just—"

Tut cut Destiny off in the middle of what she was saying. "Destiny, there you go again with all that talking. This shit is serious. We ain't got time for all this back-and-forth bullshit."

Tut immediately had Destiny's attention as she hung on to every word he was saying.

"Destiny, this is what's up. Brazil is snitching, so we gotta stop the prostitution shit until we deal with her ass. She talking to the cops, so she gotta go. That's it. Now, you either riding wit' us on this, or you're not. And if you are riding wit' us, then we need you to help us take this bitch out," Tut explained.

"Take her out? You mean, kill her?"

"Yes, Destiny," I shouted as the bass coming from the club was vibrating louder and louder in my office. "And I'll keep it totally one hundred—If you got a problem with helping us take her out, then that to me says yo' ass might be snitching too."

Destiny stood up from the couch and she paced around my office, smiling a very nervous smile. "Wow! I ain't expect this shit."

"Look, Destiny, I know what you and Brazil had planned, and I know you wanna step up your hustle game. I understand that. So here's the thing, you help us out on this, and you got my word that, me and you, we'll be partners in this club right here that you standing in. That's my word!" I said, lying to her.

Destiny blew out some air from her lungs, but she didn't say anything.

I knew that I had to keep her under pressure. So I didn't let up. "Here's the deal. We gonna walk outta this office, go out there and drink and mix it up, and party and have a good time. And when we leave here, it'll be like five in the morning. We'll shoot over to your crib in Rockaway, chill there for a minute, and then we gonna go and check that bitch Brazil and lay her ass down. That's it," I coldly said. I then grabbed my tray of coke and did another line.

Destiny had a look on her face a cat who'd swallowed a canary. I could tell that she was scared and didn't have the heart to go through with killing somebody, but I didn't give a shit. I was gonna hawk her the whole night so she couldn't try no slick shit up in the club.

I wasn't gonna let her front on my watch. She was either gonna help me take out Brazil first thing the next morning, or else her ass was gonna end up missing.

Chapter Four

Brazil

I figured that Destiny would be getting back home from the club at around six in the morning. But when it reached six thirty and she hadn't come back home yet, I started to get nervous and decided to call her. Her cell phone kept ringing out to voicemail, and I was really wondering what was up.

It was the last week of school, and Angie could have missed a day of school with no problem. I was considering not letting her go to school that day because if I left Destiny's apartment I wouldn't have been able to let myself back in. And I didn't want to go back to my house until Vegas got back in town.

But Angie was insisting on going to school so that she wouldn't miss some kiddie party that her class had planned for that day. So I got up and started to get her ready for school. By seven thirty I still hadn't heard from Destiny, and against my better judgment, I jumped in my Range Rover and headed to Rosedale to drop Angie off to school. Angie hated when I walked her all the way to the entryway of the school. She always insisted that I only walk her to the corner of the school, which was about fifty yards from the entrance door.

That particular day was no different. When I reached near her school I parked my truck on the corner of 253rd Street and 148th Avenue and I got out with her and walked her a few yards. I kissed her on the cheek. "I love you," I said to her.

"I love you too, Mommy." Angie strolled off looking so cute with her book bag strapped on to her shoulders.

I would always stand and watch her to make sure that she made it into the school safely, and that day was no different. As I stood and watched her walk off, I glanced to my left and I could have sworn that I'd seen Destiny's royal blue X-Type Jaguar drive by, but I wasn't sure. I stared really hard to see which direction the Jaguar was headed.

"Mommy!" Angie yelled, distracting me and redirecting my attention.

"What's the matter?" I asked as I walked toward her.

"Can Daddy pick me up from school today?"

"I'm not sure if he'll be here in time to get you, but if not, I'll pick you up and take you to see him later, okay?"

"Okay," she answered and then trotted off and into the school.

I turned around and walked back toward my truck, and just as I was about to step into the driver's seat, I heard someone calling my name.

"Brazil! Yo, Brazil, hol' up."

I turned and looked but I didn't see anybody. I felt like I was buggin' out, but I was sure that I'd heard somebody calling me.

Just as I turned on the ignition and fiddled with the remote control to my CD player, I saw Destiny's car driving up to mine, her driver's-side window parallel with mine. Her window began to slowly roll down.

I rolled down my window. I smiled. "I knew I wasn't trippin'. I—"

Before I could finish my sentence, I saw Destiny raise a black handgun, and without saying anything, she just started firing. *Bow! Bow! Bow! Bow!*

Instinctively I covered my head with my forearms and my hands and ducked for cover while desperately trying to squeeze my body down near the brake and the gas pedals. I screamed out in both fear and in pain as I could feel slugs entering my body one by one. My legs and my back both felt like they were on fire.

Then all of a sudden the rapid gunfire ceased, and I heard what sounded like two sets of cars screeching off.

"Oh God! Ahhh! Shhhit!" I howled and winced in pain. My body began to shake and tremble, and I coughed up globs of blood.

Rick Ross' CD came on and his music began to blare out of the speakers of my truck. I was struggling to get up and get out of the truck, afraid that more shots were about to come my way. All of my energy was fast leaving my body. I reached and grabbed the door handle and pulled it with the little energy I had left, and the door opened halfway.

All of a sudden I felt tremendously dizzy, and everything seemed as if it was spinning around at a hundred miles an hour. I could hear people screaming, and it sounded as if they were coming to my aid. But as I managed to get just my torso and my arms out of the truck, I had a strong feeling that my life was about to end right there on that street corner.

"*I love you too, Mommy.*" The image of my daughter preparing to walk into her school and her pretty little voice telling me that she loved me was the last thing that popped into my head before I blacked out and my body went limp.

Chapter Five

Essence

King Tut was riding shotgun inside of Destiny's Jaguar as a backup shooter, just in case Destiny fronted and decided not to pull the trigger. So I drove alone in my Navigator and followed closely behind Destiny's car as we sped away from the crime scene.

When we reached the town of Laurelton, about a mile and a half away from the shooting, I called Tut on his cell phone.

"Tut, tell her to pull over so you can get in my car and let's bounce," I shouted into the phone. My adrenaline was pumping and I was amped. But I can't front, I was nervous like a muthafucka. I was relieved that the whole ordeal with Brazil was over. I had to give it up to Destiny. She had more balls than I thought.

We reached the back streets of Laurelton and were on the corner of a residential block that was situated behind a supermarket, which was where both of our cars came to a stop. Tut quickly jumped out of Destiny's car, ran around to the passenger side of my car, and hopped in.

I pulled up to the side of Destiny and yelled out the window to her, "Just bounce. Wipe your prints off the gun and toss it somewhere. We gonna holla at you later." I watched her pull off. She had an uneasy look of worry on her face that I had never seen her display. Usually she looked cocky and always kept a stank, eye-rolling look about her.

Destiny took off and sped toward Laurelton Parkway. She blew the stop sign at the corner of 133rd Avenue and entered the Belt Parkway, which ran parallel to Laurelton Parkway. I followed her because I wanted to see what direction she was heading in.

"Yo, she caught her first body," Tut exclaimed.

"So she actually pulled the trigger?" I asked for confirmation, since I hadn't actually been inside the car with them.

"No doubt, that was all her. My burner ain't never leave my waistband."

Now that we were in the jungle of the Parkway, I was finally able to exhale and crack a smile because I knew me and Tut were in the clear, in terms of law enforcement. I had been parked down the block when Destiny pulled the trigger, so I wasn't too concerned about anyone having seen my license plate number. I just didn't want the cops rolling on us until Tut was out of Destiny's car. Thankfully, everything was unfolding just the way I'd wanted it to.

"Dumb bitch!" I shouted over the music that was playing inside of my truck while I reached for my BlackBerry. "You fuck my man and then sit up and smile in my face and kiss me on the cheek and shit, like everything is all good? Who the fuck you think you dealing wit'?" I turned my music off completely and dialed 9-1-1.

"9-1-1. What is your emergency?" the operator asked.

"Yeah, hi, I was just near an elementary school in Rosedale and I saw someone shooting into another car and they drove off. I followed the car and got the license plate, but I don't wanna give my name or anything like that. I don't wanna get involved like that," I said, trying my hardest to project a sense of urgency and nervousness in my voice.

"Okay, Miss, where was the shooting?"

"In Rosedale, like near 253rd Street next to an elementary school."

"Is anyone hurt?"

"Yeah, I think so. There was a lot of shots," I replied, still tailing Destiny as she drove in her car.

"Okay, we'll get someone out there right away. Now you said you saw the shooter drive off in a car? Can you tell me the make and model of the car that the shooter drove off in?"

"Yeah, that's what I'm saying, I'm following the car right now, but I can't get too close. I don't wanna get involved like that."

"Okay, give me your exact location. And can you get close enough to the car to read off the license plate number to me?"

"The car just exited the Belt Parkway at Cross Bay Boulevard, going north. It's a royal blue Jaguar with the license plate DKB-2922."

"Miss, can I get a name and a contact number for you?"

I simply ignored her last question and pressed the end button on my BlackBerry, ending the phone conversation, and headed back in the other direction on the Belt Parkway toward my plush Bayside home.

"Checkmate, bitches!" I said out loud. I smiled and looked over at my boo, King Tut, who was reclined all the way back in the passenger seat. I puckered up my full lips and blew him a kiss. I couldn't wait to get back to my crib so I could sex his brains out and relieve some of the stress I was feeling.

Chapter Six

Destiny

Before I left the club with Essence and King Tut, I'd made up my mind to go through with the plan to take out Brazil. Consciously I knew that I didn't have it in me to kill her, but I was in a tough position because, although I was cool with her, she was a snitch. I had verified that with my own eyes. So I had to do what I had to do because I didn't want to get indicted on some bullshit, thanks to her snake ass. I loaded up on liquor and weed to the point where I was as high as a kite. Without a doubt it was definitely all the liquor and the weed that took me out of my sane mind and gave me the courage to go through with the hit.

But by the time I made it to Cross Bay Boulevard and was heading toward my apartment to sort things out, my intoxicated state had completely worn off, and the adrenaline that had been flowing through my body had also left me. The reality of what I had done was starting to kick in big time. I couldn't believe what I had done as the whole scene of me pulling up to Brazil's truck and pumping sixteen bullets into her Range Rover kept replaying in my mind. I could vividly see the frightened look and sheer terror on her face when I raised my gun from my lap and started firing.

As the red light that I had been sitting at turned green, I asked myself, *Destiny, what the hell did you just do?*

Just as I was contemplating that question, I looked in my rearview mirror and saw two police cars quickly approaching in my direction at a high rate of speed without their sirens on. My heart sank to my feet, and my pupils suddenly dilated. I instantly became nervous, but thankfully both of the police cars whizzed right by me.

I slowly ran my left hand down my face and I exhaled in relief. "Whooooshhh!" I said as I shook my head.

But no sooner did my heart rate return to normal than I saw another police car approaching me from behind. That cop car also didn't have its siren on, but the cop came right up behind my car and flashed his lights in an attempt to pull me over.

"Ahh shit!" I yelled out loud into the car. I abruptly turned off the radio so that I could hear what was going on and concentrate more clearly on the drama at hand.

I reached under my seat and grabbed the 9 mm that I'd used to shoot Destiny, and then without hesitation I hit the accelerator. I was about a half-mile from the Cross Bay Bridge, and my brain raced trying to decide if I should make a U-turn and head in the other direction on Cross Bay Boulevard and try to outrun the cops that way, or if I should keep going straight and try to make it across the bridge and attempt to lose them like that.

With more cop cars approaching me from behind, I slammed my foot on the accelerator and headed full speed toward the bridge. My palms were sweaty as hell, but my hands gripped the steering wheel tighter than a vise grip.

My cell phone began ringing off the hook, but I had no time to think about answering it, as my car reached speeds of ninety miles an hour. Before I could blink I was nearing the bridge's tollbooth plaza, and there was a ton of traffic and cop cars everywhere.

"Fuck!" I screamed. *Think, think, think!* I urged myself. My body started to tremble, and I started to hyperventilate.

Things were looking bleak for me, but I knew that I had to at least ditch the gun. I swerved the car fiercely to the left and then slammed on the brakes, and my Jaguar came to a screeching halt. I burst open my driver's door and took off running. I was trying my hardest to at least make it to the base of the bridge so that I could toss the gun into the water.

Cars honked their horns and cursed and yelled at me for nearly causing multiple accidents, but I didn't care about that. All I cared about was getting away from the six cops who were chasing me on foot. Unfortunately I hadn't had time to ditch the Roberto Cavalli high-heel shoes I was wearing, making my attempt to flee on foot a very feeble one.

"Get the fuck on the ground!" one of the cops yelled at me as he dove and tackled me.

"Uggghhh!" I cried out in pain as my body came crashing to the concrete face first. I was in instant agonizing pain from my face scraping the ground.

But I had no time to worry about the stinging sensations or how my face looked as I wrestled with the plainclothes cop in an attempt to break free from his clutches. "Get the fuck off of me!" I screamed at him.

The cop who wrestled with me yelled to his fellow officers, "Grab the gun! Grab the gun!"

Someone grabbed the gun from my hand, and within a split second there were about five cops on top of me, trying to subdue me.

"Ahhhh!" I hollered. One of the cops twisted my right

arm behind my back so forcefully, I was sure that he had broken it.

Another cop grabbed hold of my left arm and twisted that one behind my back as well, and then I felt handcuffs being applied to my both of my wrists. The cuffs were so tight, they were cutting into my flesh and bones.

I lay on the ground at the base of the Cross Bay Bridge, my face and wrist throbbing, my body and mind feeling defeated, as what looked like a million cop cars continually arrived at the scene.

I had almost made it safely to my apartment that overlooked the serene waters of Rockaway Beach. In fact, I was less than five minutes from home. But as I lay handcuffed, in pain, face first on the concrete, I knew that it would probably be a long-ass time before I would be able to freely make it back home to my apartment.

Chapter Seven

Essence

It was the middle of July 2006. Destiny had been locked up on Rikers Island for approximately three weeks. She had been blowing up my phone on an everyday basis and I knew that I had to visit her as soon as possible. Actually, I didn't have to go see her, but I knew that going would be a smart strategic move, so I was planning on seeing her in a day or two.

Brazil, that bitch, had been hit with six out of sixteen bullets, and somehow her ass was still clinging to life. She had been shot twice in both the back and in the stomach, and once in the leg and in the arm. Although she was in critical condition and in a medically induced coma, the doctors were optimistic that she was gonna pull through. I couldn't believe it. I was gonna have to figure out a way to totally crush her ass.

But for the time being I had other things to concern myself with. Primarily I had to worry about paying Shabazz the $20,000 that he wanted for getting me the fake affidavit that I'd used to accuse Brazil of being a snitch.

Shabazz was an undercover cop for the New York Police Department. He worked out of the Bronx on different kinds of undercover tasks forces, and although he was only thirty years old, he had a high rank and a lot of pull within the police department because of who his father was. His father was like the number three man in the police department behind the Police Commissioner and the Deputy Commissioner.

Shabazz could have been the poster child for crooked cops. He was as corrupt and as dirty as they came. But he was very good at covering up his tracks and he was also super smart. So he really didn't have much to worry about, in terms of ever getting bagged for abusing his authority. And it was that abuse of authority that let him get away with all of the underhanded shit that he did.

Shabazz and I met back in like 1998 when I was only twenty years old. He helped to lock up my former Dominican boyfriend named Kenny. Shabazz was so good at what he did when it came to investigating Kenny that almost single-handedly based on the evidence that he had compiled, the district attorney was able to get Kenny convicted on a "kingpin statute" and send him away for life.

But the wild part of it all was that Shabazz had rolled with me and Kenny and Kenny's whole crew on a regular basis, and all of us that were a part of Kenny's crew had no idea that he was a cop. That's just how good he was. In fact, it wasn't until three years later in 2001 when I had opened up Promiscuous Girl, did I find out that he was a cop.

Shabazz came through the club, and although it had been three years since I had last seen him, I immediately recognized him.

"Shabazz!" I screamed and ran up to him and hugged him and kissed him.

"Oh shit, Essence. What's up, ma?" he replied.

From there, me and Shabazz caught up on old times. And while we were talking and getting caught up with each other, he was upfront with me, telling me that he knew I owned the club and that was why he had come by. He wanted to know if he and I could talk in private about some things.

Immediately I thought that Shabazz was gonna try to fast-talk me or smooth-talk me into letting him help me run the club. But what he did was he took me into my private office and shocked the hell out of me when he showed me his gold badge and laid everything out to me, as far as him being a cop and how long he had been a cop and all of that.

"You bullshitting me, or are you dead-ass?" I asked.

"*Rachel Wright*, I ain't bullshitting," Shabazz answered, letting me know that he knew my government name. That was something that I never let anyone know, especially not my last name.

I cracked a half-smile as I paced in my office. "So you a fuckin' cop?"

Shabazz nodded his head and looked at me, but he didn't say anything.

"You know I'm bugging, right?" I asked him.

Shabazz had a dead serious look on his face. "Look, I'ma be straight-up. I wanna kick it with you later 'cause I think me and you could work something out."

"Work something out like what?"

"Essence, do I gotta spell it out for you? I got a badge and a gun, ma. And my whole crew got guns and badges. You feel me?"

I was street-smart, so I read between the lines and caught on really quick. And in the days and weeks that followed that impromptu reuniting with Shabazz, he and I worked out an arrangement that made Promiscuous Girl virtually untouchable.

For $15,000 a month, Shabazz assured me that, regardless of any community complaints and all of the legal type of drama and headaches that came with running a strip club, he would be able to get Promiscuous Girl a pass and a heads-up on any drama or investigations that came our way or was headed our way.

Fast-forward to five years later, and the deal that Shabazz and I had worked out was still in effect. It had worked out better than I could have ever imagined. The thing though that made it work so well was the fact that he and I both knew how to keep our fucking mouths shut. Nobody, not even Tut, knew that Shabazz was a cop. The only thing that people knew was that he was a bouncer who sometimes worked the door, just like all of the other bouncers.

During those five years Shabazz had also helped me move countless pounds of marijuana, making drops for me to different drug dealers that I had come to know and trust from back in the days. And those same drug dealers would frequent my club on a regular basis and spend shit-loads of money.

I not only kept my mouth shut about him being a cop, but I also kept my mouth shut about the secret sexual trysts that he and I had going on for the past five years.

Without question Shabazz was definitely addicted to sex. He wanted to fuck morning noon and night, but at the same time I respected and was okay with his situation and he was okay with and respected mine.

Like when Tut came home from jail, Shabazz knew that he was gonna have to fall back a little bit. So when Tut came home, Shabazz and I worked it out to where we would meet up at the club during off-hours to fuck.

It was two o'clock in the afternoon when I met Shabazz at the club to pay him an extra $20,000. That was on top of the $15,000 that I had already given him. He'd pulled strings to get the authentic signature page from an old bullshit affidavit that Brazil had signed like two years ago on something totally unrelated to Promiscuous Girl. And once he had that, it then became just a matter of typing out the other pages to a fake affidavit and attaching it to the signature page of the real affidavit. And what we had was a signed affidavit from Brazil that looked damn believable.

Even the whole raid on my strip club had been planned and orchestrated and initiated by Shabazz. But since I knew that the raid was coming, I made sure that the club and no one in it was dirty on the night of the raid.

"I got that for you," I said to Shabazz when he walked into my office. I stood up from behind my desk wearing a white slingshot bikini and clear stilettos.

Although I had never actually stripped in a club a day in my life, Shabazz loved all that sexy exotic stripper shit like stilettos and thongs, so I would dress up in that for him.

He took the envelope of cash from me and smiled. "So you gonna dance for me, Naomi?"

Because of my height and my complexion, many people told me that I looked and acted a lot like the supermodel Naomi Campbell, so *Naomi* became Shabazz's pet name for me.

I seductively ran my fingers down Shabazz's face and chest, and then I motioned with my index finger for him to follow me. I went to the DJ booth and turned on 50 Cent's hit song "Candy Shop." Then I made my way to the bar and stood on the counter and began to dance for Shabazz.

This type of role-playing became a weekly routine for me and Shabazz. That was just the type of freaky shit that he liked doing, and I didn't mind doing it for him, if it was gonna keep him happy.

Shabazz stood about six-foot-two, and was about 200 pounds and he had a nice, toned body. For the most part, he was an average-looking dark-skin dude and he kept a low haircut that looked as if he went to the barber every day to get his shit lined. He had an average-size dick, but he knew how to work that shit. And although I liked fucking King Tut, sex with Shabazz was definitely better than with Tut because he made me cum every time, without question.

While I danced to the song, Shabazz threw hundred-dollar bills at me as he sipped on his Heineken. Before long though he had taken off his clothes and was on top of the bar, and I was sucking his dick.

I loved hearing Shabazz moan and make different sounds when I sucked his dick, but the music was so loud that I couldn't hear anything. I deep-throated him, swallowing all of his dick. I looked up at him and he looked like he was in ecstasy. I knew that he was enjoying the head that I was giving him.

When he couldn't take it any more, he guided me to stand up.

I knew that he wanted to fuck me from behind, so I turned my ass to face him and held on to one of the stripper poles and waited for him to enter me.

Shabazz hopped off the bar counter and put back on the Timberland boots that he was wearing, and then he hopped back up on the bar. I couldn't help but turn my head in his direction and laugh at him. He just had this thing where he loved to fuck in his Timbs. He pulled the thong of my bikini to the side and slid his fat dick into my wet pussy and it felt so damn good.

The music was still blasting, only now one of Lil' Kim's songs was coming through the speakers as I backed my ass up on to Shabazz's dick.

He grabbed a fistful of my hair and pulled on it, and rammed his dick as hard as he could into my pussy. I loved whenever he pulled on my hair. It was like a trigger that would instantly make me cum.

And sure enough after like ten or twenty more strokes I was cumming all over Shabazz's dick. "Oh God! You always make me feel so damn good!" I screamed out to him.

About two minutes after I came, Shabazz pulled his dick outta me. I knew that he was about to cum, so I turned around and knelt down on my knees and began sucking on his dick. It drove him crazy whenever I let him buss in my mouth, so I sucked his dick until he came right inside my throat. Shabazz let out the loudest roar, sounding like a lion when he came, holding onto my head like he was gripping a basketball or something. I slowly pulled his dick out of my mouth and looked up at him and smiled as some of his cum dripped onto my chin.

Shabazz kissed me on my cheek with his soft-ass lips. I was definitely addicted to him, but I was in love with Tut. The way I saw it, although Shabazz was my "maintenance man," I wasn't being disloyal to Tut, because me and Shabazz fucked each other based solely on a business arrangement that was in place before Tut was in the picture. Besides, Shabazz and Tut weren't close friends; they were merely associates, if that.

I had a bunch of moves to make that day, including running with Tut to Manhattan, so I had to hurry up and get dressed.

Chapter Eight

Brazil

I had been in the hospital for one complete month. For the majority of that time I had been in a medically induced coma. When I came out of it, the doctors all explained to me just how lucky I was to be alive and to not be cripple. The bullets that Destiny had pumped into my back and my stomach all came within centimeters of hitting my vital organs and my spine.

Everyone said that God must have been on my side, and maybe He was, I don't know. I do know that I had actually seen that huge bright light that everyone who has ever had a near-death experience talks about.

As far as I was concerned, it was my own will that had kept me alive. I'll admit that I was scared as hell when Destiny pulled up to my truck and started firing on me. I thought that I was dead for sure. But I remember slipping in and out of consciousness as the ambulance rushed me to the trauma unit. And inside the trauma unit, I was having an out-of-body experience. It was like one minute I would be standing behind the doctors watching them feverishly trying to save my life, and then the next minute

I would be laying on the operating table in excruciating pain.

The one thing that was certain for me was that I had convinced myself that I had to stay alive for my daughter's sake. And to check Destiny's snake ass for having shot me for no reason at all.

As I lay in my hospital bed recovering from my wounds, I realized that the gunshot wounds didn't hurt me nearly as much as Destiny had hurt me, backstabbing and betraying me the way she'd done.

Vegas was right when he explained to me, "Money changes people." He knew like I knew that the only reason Destiny had shot me was because she wanted to have the new club that we were opening all to herself. She knew where I was stashing all of my paper, and I know that she had plans to raid my stash after I was gone, so she could open the club on her own and not have to split any profits with anybody.

Unfortunately for her, she got caught before she could go though with her plan. That was her problem, not mine.

One thing was for sure—As soon as I was healthy enough and able to leave the hospital, I was gonna get revenge on both Essence and Destiny, if it was the last thing on earth I did. On the life of my daughter, both of those bitches had to bleed and feel the same pain that I was feeling. It's only right.

Chapter Nine

Destiny

I spotted Essence as soon as I walked into the visiting room. Looking like brand-new money and smelling like a bed of roses, she had on some tight white pants, a sheer all white spaghetti strap blouse with a white tube top underneath, and white open-toe high-heel shoes. Her brown skin looked flawless, and from the looks of it, she looked as if she had on a thousand-dollar wig that I had never seen before.

I, on the other hand, had on a baggy prison-issued orange jumpsuit and some black flip-flops. I had no makeup on, my hair and nails looked like shit, and the right side of my face was still pink and scabbed in several places.

I pulled out my chair and sat down across the table from her. I'd had weeks to sit in my cell and think about everything, and I was frustrated as shit. But what had pissed me off the most was the fact that both Essence and King Tut hadn't been taking my calls, and up until that point neither one of them had even visited me while I was on the Island.

"Essence, you know you on some bullshit, right?"

She tried her hardest to look concerned. "What happened to your face?"

"Don't worry about that."

She smiled. "Destiny, I gotcha. Just relax."

"Don't fuckin' tell me to relax, when you got my ass up in here not knowing what to think. Meanwhile you and Tut out there on the street living it up and shit, and y'all can't come to see my ass or take a gotdamn call from me? What the hell is that?"

"First of all, sweetie, me and Tut ain't put you in here. You fucked up and put your gotdamn self in here. Let's get that shit straight before we even proceed, okay?"

Essence continued with that damn smiley smirk on her face. I didn't respond, I just looked at her and blew out a bunch of air from my lungs. I swear to God, I was two seconds from smacking earth, wind, and fire from out of her ass.

"Now, Destiny, we ain't been taking your calls and we didn't come to see you because we ain't want no heat on our asses. We had to give shit a chance to calm down and let the heat cool off. Don't tell me you can't understand that."

"Fuck that," I said in a loud whisper. I was vexed as hell and I couldn't hold back my anger. "My money ain't right, and I'm stuck wit' a bullshit-ass lawyer that ain't doing shit for me. At least y'all coulda looked out for me on that."

Essence just cleared her throat and smiled but she didn't say anything.

"Essence, that whole deal still stands. I want half of that Promiscuous Girl money."

Essence chuckled. She looked around the room. "Oooh damn, it's hot as hell up in here. I need some water or something."

"Listen, don't try and change the subject. We had a deal, and that's why I pulled that trigger."

Essence paused and looked at me in my eyes. The smile had disappeared from her face. "Listen, that deal is off the table. Destiny, you fucked. You got your ass locked up, and Brazil is still breathing. My hands are tied. What the hell am I supposed to do?"

I closed my eyes and ran my hand down my face in frustration. With the weeks I'd had to think about everything that had gone down between me, Essence, and Brazil, I had nothing but time on my hands to think about just exactly how I was gonna get out of my predicament. I knew that I had to figure a way out of my dilemma on my own. A big part of me knew that if and when Essence showed up to see me that she would only be coming to visit me just so she could feel me out to see if I was gonna mention anything about ratting her out to the police or some shit. And as we sat and spoke, I realized she was purposely trying to provoke me to anger to see what my response would be.

See, the thing is, I might've fucked her man, but I wasn't no snitch. Snitching wasn't my way of life, so regardless of how I felt about her, at the end of the day she was right. I was where I was at because I had fucked up. And she was making it clear that I was now on my own. That was all I needed to hear because now I knew what moves I had to make.

Essence had the power, and she had the money. She was on top, and my ass was locked behind bars. I had no choice but to play things humble, but it wasn't exactly easy for me to be humble.

"What are *you* supposed to do? You know what? Don't do shit for me, Essence. You ain't gotta do shit for me. I got this," I said in a real matter-of-fact tone.

Essence looked at me. Then that annoying smirk-ass smile returned to her face. "*You ain't gotta do shit for*

me," she said in a tone that mocked me. Then she leaned
her body over the table in an effort to get closer to me and
spoke with clinched teeth. "Bitch, don't come at me with
that reverse-psychology-mind-games-bullshit. Remember,
I made your ass. Before I met you, you was up in Sue's
selling your ass to the highest bidder and living in your
mother's basement. I already did more for you than I
should have, so don't come at me with that bullshit."

I had to butt in or else I would have lost it. I smiled.
"A'ight, you got it, you got it. You can talk all that shit
'cause you know I'm locked up. It's all good. It is what it
is."

"Listen, Destiny, whether you're locked up or walking
the street, it don't matter, 'cause your ass ain't above getting touched, no matter where you at. Now what you
need to do is learn how to humble your ass and apologize
to me for fuckin' my man and smiling in my face like shit
was all good." Essence stared at me and pushed her chair
away from the table and stood up to leave.

I have to admit, she did catch me off guard with that
one, but since she had put it out there, then it was fair
game to talk about it.

"Yeah, I did fuck your man," I said as I too stood up and
stared at her. "I was fuckin' him almost every day, and you
know what? The shit was good too."

Essence licked her lips and smiled, and then a frown of
confusion appeared on her face and forehead. "That's
funny 'cause, the way Tut explained it to me, he said you
can't take no dick, you don't know how to suck a dick,
and that the sex was whack, straight up and down. Listen,
tell you what, when you get outta here, I'll teach you how
to take some dick like a real woman. Is that a'ight?"
Essence twisted her lips at me and turned to walk out.

Indescribable rage ran through my body as I watched

her walk out of the visiting room with all of her "fabulousity." I tried to calm down as I made my way back to my cell and thought about my next move. There was no way I could let that bitch chump my ass and get away with it. I had to think of something. I just had to.

Chapter Ten

Essence

It was September 2006. Two and a half months had passed since Brazil had been shot. And word on the street was that she had been released from the hospital less than a week ago. Her chump-ass baby father and some of his boys had come to Promiscuous Girl on some rah-rah thug shit about two weeks ago. Although they'd never made it past security and the bouncers, they were threatening to do harm to me and to Tut. And as they'd put it, they "would shoot up the whole fuckin' club and everybody inside of it" if they had to.

Tut and I both knew that Vegas was all bark and no bite. The proof in the pudding was that it had been more than two months since his baby's mother had almost been shot dead in the street right near his daughter's school, more than two months since me and Tut had gone inside his baby's mother's crib and disrespected her, something that I was sure Brazil had told him about, and yet he'd never retaliated. The dude was a pussy.

Regardless of the fact that Vegas was a punk, I still

made sure to beef up security at the club. I also started traveling with my own personal security in the form of off-duty cops. In the same way that no one knew that Shabazz was a cop, no one knew that I was rolling with off-duty cops, because the one or two dudes that I had riding shotgun with me always looked liked your average everyday thugged-out niggas.

I knew that Brazil would be seeking some form of revenge as soon as she came home from the hospital. And since Destiny was locked up and she couldn't get revenge on her, I knew she would definitely come gunning for me. And, sure enough, I was right.

As I pulled up to Tut's crib on Long Street just off of Foch Boulevard, Kwame, the off-duty cop who was riding with me, asked, "You recognize that black car over there?"

"Nah, it don't look familiar," I said as I left the ignition on and me and him sat in front of Tut's crib, the car idling.

"Let's just chill here for a minute. The windows on that car are tinted, the car got out of state plates, and the engine is running. It don't seem right. Let's just see if somebody comes out the car."

Kwame and I both sat quiet in my truck for a few minutes, and no one ever emerged from the black Dodge Magnum.

"Yo, let me call Tut and see if it's one of his people chilling outside and waiting for him or something," I said as I began calling Tut's phone.

I didn't know if Tut was in the crib or what, because his car wasn't parked in his driveway. Instead there was another car in his driveway that I didn't recognize. I was almost sure that he was home, yet I got no answer. It just seemed strange to me, so I called back. Still I got no answer. Instantly my heart rate picked up.

"Yo, he ain't picking up the phone," I said to Kwame. "I don't like that. I think something is up."

"A'ight, this is what we gonna do. We both gonna get

out the truck and start making our way to Tut's front door, and if anybody approaches us, I'm reaching for my burner, just so that they know that I'm strapped."

I turned off the ignition. "Okay cool."

Kwame and I both exited my truck at the same time and began walking toward Tut's house.

"Essence!" someone yelled from across the street in the direction of the black Magnum.

Kwame and I both turned to look, and we saw Brazil, Vegas, and one of his boys emerge from the Magnum.

Brazil, her silky, jet-black hair pulled back into a ponytail, still looked stunningly beautiful in the face, but she looked really skinny in her Sean John sweat suit. Vegas and his boy both had on jeans and Timbs, and his boy, probably a Blood, had a red bandanna that covered his face.

Kwame and I both stopped. Kwame positioned his large linebacker-looking frame in front of me.

"Is there a problem?" he asked.

"Yeah, we got a muthafuckin' problem!" The dude in the red bandanna lifted his shirt to show us that he was holding heat.

Kwame didn't identify himself as a cop, but he immediately pulled his gun from his waistband and aimed it right at Brazil and her crew, catching them all off guard. "So how the fuck y'all wanna handle this shit?" he asked. "Reach for your shit and I'll have you leaking right here all over this cement," Kwame said, sounding real gangsta.

I was nervous, but I knew that I was in good hands with Kwame. Plus, I could tell that Kwame had intimidated Brazil and Vegas, because they both immediately backed up as if they wanted to run for cover when Kwame pulled his gun.

"Look at this bitch-ass nigga," the Blood said to Vegas and Brazil. "I should blast his ass right now."

"Test my gangsta if you wanna," Kwame said, his gun locked on the dude.

"Essence, why you hiding behind your boy?" Brazil asked.

I didn't respond to her because the situation didn't call for talking. If they was 'bout it, then all they had to do was start bussin' they heat. No need for words.

"Tell me what the fuck y'all wanna do," Kwame said, sounding cocky as a muthafucka. "Y'all wanna shoot this shit out or what?"

"Fuck this! She pussy just like I thought." Brazil started backing off and signaling for Vegas and his man to follow them.

"Essence, go inside the crib. I'ma wait out here to make sure these niggas don't try nothing slick."

I turned and walked toward Tut's side door. I looked over my shoulder as I walked. I could see that Brazil didn't even have all of her physical strength. She more than likely should have still been in a bed somewhere. But from that point on I knew that if she got out of her sick bed to come hunting for me, then she wasn't gonna stop until she felt that she'd gotten vengeance. So her ass had to be totally eliminated. I just had to figure out exactly how I was gonna handle her annoying ass.

I unlocked Tut's side door. He usually chilled in his living room watching ESPN or some kind of sports, so that's where I immediately headed.

"Tut, you believe that Brazil and her frail, sick ass is outside wit' Vegas and some Blood dude?" I said as I walked into the living room.

Although the TV was on ESPN and music was coming from the stereo speakers, Tut wasn't in the living room. I chuckled when I realized I had been talking to myself. I headed upstairs to see if he was there. As I made my way up the stairs, I heard something that just didn't sound right, so I paused. *What the fuck?* I thought to myself.

I slowly tiptoed the rest of the way up the stairs and approached Tut's bedroom. When I was finally at the door of Tut's bedroom, I almost collapsed from disbelief as I looked and saw Tut, his pants down around his ankles, fucking some dude in the ass while the dude lay bent over on his king-size bed.

"Uggggh, Ugggghhh, Ughhh!" Tut grunted as he pumped his dick in and out of some muscle-bound dude's asshole.

The dude who was receiving the dick was gasping like a straight bitch, with every stroke that he received.

"Tut, what the fuck is going on!" I yelled.

I entered the room and ran right up on the action so I could see everything up close and personal and confirm exactly what the hell it was I didn't want to believe that my eyes were telling me. And, sure enough, Tut was standing there with his big hard-ass dick up inside the dude's ass, raw dog at that.

"Oh shit! Essence, what the fuck are you doing here?"

Tut and the other dude both started scrambling to pull up their pants and cover themselves up.

"Joystick?" I asked in disbelief, as I realized that I recognized the dude Tut was fucking. He was this male exotic dancer that went by the name of *Joystick*. "Oh my God! I think I'm gonna throw the hell up." I grabbed my stomach. I literally felt sick.

Tut came up to me and grabbed hold of my hand. "Baby, this ain't nothing."

"Nigga, get your hands off of me!" I yanked my hand away from Tut's grip and headed downstairs.

"Where you going?"

"Don't worry about where I'm going. I'm just getting the

hell outta here," I shouted and kept it moving as quickly as I could.

When I reached the kitchen and was a few feet away from exiting from the side door, Tut grabbed me.

"Essence, stop buggin', 'cause it ain't that serious!" he shouted, gripping me up.

"Tut, get your fuckin' hands off of me."

He just gripped me tighter and then tried to get gangsta on me. "Essence, you ain't going nowhere. Leave this house and I'll knock your fuckin' teeth out."

"Was you ever gonna tell me you was a fuckin' homo thug?" I asked Tut as I tried to wrestle myself free from his grip. "What? Did you get turned out in jail or some shit and that's what gotcha like this? King muthafuckin' Tut, a homo thug?"

WHACK!

Tut smacked me so hard across my face, I spun around and fell face first to his granite-tiled kitchen floor. His slap dazed me for a minute, and it took me some time to gather myself.

As I stood up I could hear the front door opening, and Joystick yelled out to Tut that he would holla at him later.

Tut didn't respond. Instead he focused his attention on me. He grabbed me by my throat with his right hand and slammed me against the wall.

I kicked and punched and slapped and did whatever I could do to loosen his grip on my throat, but I was obviously having absolutely no effect on him and his twenty-two-inch arms.

"Nothing goes past me and you and the walls of this house, you understand that shit?"

When I didn't respond, Tut just increased the pressure around my neck. "You understand me!" he hollered.

I knew that I was in danger of dying right there on the

spot if I didn't comply with him. I felt like I was going to pass out, as I literally could get no air into my lungs. I nodded my head in agreement, and when he saw that, he loosened his grip and slammed me to the ground. As soon as I hit his kitchen floor for the second time, I began gasping for air. I managed to get about two exaggerated gasps of air, but my circulation was soon cut off again by Tut and his size thirteen Nike Air, which he planted on my throat, pinning me to the floor.

"I ain't Destiny, and I ain't Brazil or any of these other little bitches that you control. Essence, you know my stats, and you know how I get down. Test me if you want to, but I swear on everything that, if you do, I'll have your ass chopped the fuck up!"

Then to further show his dominance, he picked me up off the ground and ripped off my pants and my panties so that he could fuck me.

I tried to fight him off, but there was no use. He was much stronger than me and madder than a deranged pit bull.

Tut flung me across the kitchen, and then he ran up to me and bent me over the kitchen table and began massaging his dick, to get it erect. As soon as he was hard, he stuck his same damn dirty dick inside of me that he had just been fucking Joystick with. I howled in pain as his dick ripped through my dry pussy.

I needed this drama like I needed a hole in my head. As I got raped by Tut, I didn't care about trying to figure out what I should do about my newfound revelation that he was a homo thug, nor was I concerned about trying to figure out exactly how to take care of Brazil and her pesky ass. Nah, the only thing that I was thinking and feeling was pain, devastation, and humiliation.

Tut had violated me in the worst way imaginable. After

he had finished raping me, he shot a load of cum all over my face, threw me to the ground, and spat on me. He screamed, "Bitch!" before stomping off and going about his business and leaving me disgraced, brutalized, and scrambling on the floor in shock and horror.

Chapter Eleven

Destiny

I wasn't expecting any visitors, so when I was told that I had a visitor, I immediately thought that it was my Spanish homegirl from Washington Heights, Cathy, my most loyal and regular visitor since I'd been on Rikers Island. To my complete shock and surprise, when I reached the visiting room I saw that it was King Tut who had come to pay me a visit.

Tut looked good. I could tell that he'd been hitting the weights, because his chest and his arms looked extra swollen through the button-up shirt that he had on.

I didn't know whether to be angry or to be happy. Consciously, I knew that I should be angry with him, but it was hard to deny that part of me was genuinely excited to see him.

"You finally came," I said as I sat down in front of him.

Tut nodded his head before telling me that I looked good. My face had finally healed up, and the scabs were all completely gone, so I was feeling more confident about my looks.

"I know I shoulda been here for you and I wasn't. I ain't making no excuses or nothing like that, but as a man, I apologize. Straight up, I apologize." Tut adjusted himself in his chair.

I didn't know what to think or say, but I did know that I should be suspicious.

"I don't know, Tut. I mean, I thought we were tighter than that, but maybe I was wrong. Maybe it really was just about the sex for you."

"Destiny, of course, you know it wasn't just about no pussy for me, and I'm sure that it wasn't just about the dick for you. But we both knew going in that I had my situation with Essence."

"So, be honest, she kept you away from here, didn't she?"

"Destiny, I'm my own man, you know that. I already told you I ain't gonna make no excuses. But what I will say is, you know how manipulating Essence can be, right?"

I nodded my head and gazed at him, just wishing that he could break me off some of that dick. I was so horny and backed up from not having had any dick in months that if Tut had just blew on me, I would probably have cum on myself right there as I sat in that chair.

"Destiny, she crossed you."

"Who? Essence?"

"Yeah, that's her nature, and that's what I'm finding out. She ain't really who I thought she was. I'm starting to see a lot of shit different. Like on the real, for real, I be wishing that I had just rocked wit'chu and that she wasn't even in the picture."

I was trying my hardest to figure out where all of this was coming from. "Tut, did you tell her that you was fuckin' me?"

Tut nodded his head.

"Why?" I asked, confused.

Tut didn't respond.

"She was in here talking real greasy when she came to see me. So you did tell her that sex with me was whack and that I couldn't take no dick?"

"Hell, no. What the fuck are you talking about?"

"Forget about that. Just tell me what you mean, she crossed me. I don't understand what you mean by that."

"Destiny, just think about how shit went down. Essence tells you that Brazil is trying to snake you and then she gets you to take out Brazil and you end up getting knocked the same day? That shit don't seem strange to you?"

Not only did what Tut was detailing to me seem strange, but it had been the thing that I had been obsessing over since I had been in joint. I knew that something wasn't right about the way things had gone down, but I never had any confirmation. I had a feeling where Tut was going with his words.

"Tut, don't tell me you co-signed on that bitch setting me the fuck up?"

Tut just looked at me.

I closed my eyes, and my fuse instantly blew. I was getting ready to curse Tut's ass out, but he spoke up before I could say anything.

"Destiny, you know I would never cosign on no shit like that. All that came out in the wash when she found out that I was fucking you. She the one that called five-O on you and gave your license plate and told them where you live at and the whole nine yards."

I covered my face with both of my hands and I exhaled all of the air that was inside of my lungs. I began to hyperventilate as I looked at Tut and tried my hardest to read him. I was also panicking over the fact that Essence had done me so dirty.

Tut went on to explain to me that he still cared about me and told me how he was gonna come see me every week, and he went on and on. But, deep down inside, I sensed that he was being phony and felt like he was blowing smoke up my ass. I didn't know exactly what was up, but I knew that he was lying about not having known beforehand that Essence had set me up all along, and that he was probably the one who'd helped her to carry out the plan.

The thing that I couldn't figure out was why he would be coming to Rikers Island to tell me that Essence had crossed me. That just didn't make sense to me. Regardless, I couldn't sit there and be phony and look him in his face like things were all good. I small-talked him for about two more minutes before making up an excuse for why I had to go back to my cell. And after he updated me on Brazil's health status, we parted ways.

Two weeks had passed since Tut had come to visit me that initial time on Rikers Island. And during those two weeks I was on the brink of blacking out with anger. I was so frustrated about being locked up and not being able to get back at Essence, I thought I would die. I tried my best to not let my emotions get the better of me, but unfortunately my emotions were winning out and my sanity was suffering. All the same I came up with a plan that I was gonna soon carry out, and I didn't let any of the other inmates in on it.

During the first week in October 2006, I was scheduled to make a court appearance in Queens County Criminal Court, which was located in the Kew Gardens section of Queens, not too far from the Promiscuous Girl strip club on Hillside Avenue in the Jamaica section of Queens.

I had to be in court at two PM on a Thursday afternoon, so I was transported to the courthouse along with ten other inmates. We rode together on a Department of Corrections bus that was driven by a white male corrections officer.

It was approximately eleven thirty in the morning, and as the bus traveled briskly down the Grand Central Parkway, I psyched myself up.

Just do it, Destiny. You can't front on me now, I said to myself. *A'ight, a'ight. I'm good. I'm good. I got this,* I said as the bus exited the parkway and the courthouse came in full view. The exit ramp was full of cars, causing the bus to repeatedly stop and go. But that proved to be a blessing in disguise for me.

Thankfully for me I wasn't considered a troublemaker, and so I wasn't shackled to any of the other inmates as we rode together on the bus. So with my hands cuffed behind my back and my heart jumping out of my chest, I stood up. I quickly used my double-jointed ability to raise my arms behind me and rotate my shoulders forward in a way that the average person just cannot do. In the process I was able to bring my cuffed hands and my arms to the front of my body.

The side and back windows of the bus all had bolted metal gates on them, so trying to make it through one of those windows wasn't an option. But the front windshield of the bus did not have any bars or metal gates on them, and it wasn't made of bulletproof glass, so I knew that I could make it through that window. Without hesitation I bolted toward the front of the bus screaming and dove shoulder first through the windshield of the bus. I had done things so fast, I was sure that I had shocked the hell out of everybody that and no one probably had time to figure out what had just happened.

Thankfully for me, traffic hadn't yet started to move as I came crashing to the cement and shattered glass rained down on me. *Get up! Get up! Get up!* I urged myself. I sprang to my feet and just started running in between cars as fast as I could. I must have looked like an orange blur because I was running faster than a track star in my bright orange prison suit and sneakers.

I came upon Queens Boulevard, one of the busiest streets in all of New York, and bolted across the Boulevard, almost getting run over in the process, but I knew that I would get bagged if I stopped or hesitated for even a split second.

After successfully making it across Queens Boulevard, I saw a bunch of stores and high-rise apartment buildings and decided to head toward one of the buildings. I headed straight for the tallest one.

When I got closer to it, I saw a large brown garbage dumpster. I ran to the dumpster and was just about to attempt to lift the lid, but then I saw a door that looked as if it led to the basement of the building. I decided to try it to see if it was open. I twisted the knob and pulled on the door and it opened. No sooner than I had got the door open did I hear police sirens that seemed as if they were coming from every direction. I went into the building and slammed the door shut behind me.

I was so nervous, I could literally hear every breath that I breathed. *Destiny, calm down and just think.* I surveyed where I was at and decided to go down a set of steps that was just off to my right. After I made it down the steps, I realized that I was in fact in the basement of the apartment building. I came across a door that read *Superintendent.* As quietly as possible, I crept past that door and I came upon two other doors, both of which were locked. I then checked another door and that door was open. I peeked inside and saw a huge round iron tub, which I figured was the boiler. I went all the way into the room and closed the door behind me and quickly walked around to the opposite side of the boiler, where if someone were to walk inside that room they wouldn't have immediately seen me.

I sat down on the filthy floor next to the boiler and tried my hardest to relax and calm down. I hoped with everything that I had that I wouldn't get busted.

Chapter Twelve

Brazil

After me, Vegas, and his boy had stepped to Essence and her security person, I realized that I was going about things the wrong way. It was like I was trying to attack a dog that was awake, and I realized that it would be smarter to attack a sleeping dog.

Literally as I sat in my grandmother's crib nursing my wounds, watching TV with my daughter, and thinking about the best scheme to catch Essence off guard, the TV program that I was watching was interrupted with a breaking news story about an escaped prisoner.

"You son of a bitch!" I screamed at the television. I was shocked and in disbelief when I realized that it was Destiny the news program was reporting on.

No more than ten minutes has passed by and my phone was ringing off the hook with people calling me and informing me that Destiny had managed to escape. Everyone, from the District Attorney's office, to detectives, to some of my stripper friends, to Vegas, had called me. My response to everyone was all the same. I responded calmly and with no drama or fear.

The reason that I was able to respond like that was because I came to understand that the only power that either Destiny or Essence had over me was the power that I gave them. And I knew that if I spent all day worrying about them and what moves they were making and wondering if they were planning on coming after me, then all that would've done was leave me paralyzed.

Only attack a dog when it's sleeping, I reminded myself. I stood from my grandmother's couch and watched and listened to the television reporter. *Brazil, just do you and don't worry about that bitch. If she don't get caught, you'll catch her slippin', just like you'll catch Essence out there slippin'.*

Truth be told, I wanted revenge in the worst way, but I also knew that the best revenge that I could possibly get would be to start my strip club by myself as I had long been planning to do, and to get that shit off the ground and to get it poppin'.

From the day that I had emerged from my medically induced coma and was well enough to have visitors, I was working on the plans for my new club. That's just how focused I was. In fact, while I was in the hospital, the name *Magic City* kept coming into my mind, like it was a revelation of some sorts. I knew that was what I had to name my strip club.

All of the chicks I knew who were strippers and had come to visit me in the hospital were all told about my plans for my new strip club, and they all promised me that if I made it home and got the club up and running, they would come through for me and work the club for me.

So all of the pieces to the puzzle had been coming together. Vegas had been handling all of the legal shit for me, having lawyers file all of the necessary legal paperwork and getting the licenses I would need to be totally legit. I had about one hundred and twenty grand stashed, and while it wasn't enough to purchase a location, it was more than enough for me to get a lease for a location that I had found.

If all went according to plan, in a matter of weeks Magic City would be open for business on the corner of Rockaway and Farmers Boulevard in an industrial area located right near JFK Airport. It was a dynamite location with tons of traffic flowing past it. But the best thing that I liked about the location was that it would be close enough to Promiscuous Girl where Essence would have no choice but to feel the negative effects that Magic City would have on her club.

I couldn't wait to get it on and poppin'.

Chapter Thirteen

Essence

Ididn't know what the hell to do about Tut being a got-damn homo thug. I had so many conflicting emotions that I was fighting. On one hand, I was pissed off that he'd raped me the way he did, and on the other, I still genuinely cared about him. I was scared for being put in a position where I could be walking around with HIV or AIDS and not even know it. But when I thought about how good the dick was, it kinda helped to smooth shit over in my mind.

The bottom line, though, was that I had a reputation to uphold, and although I wasn't gonna out King Tut's homo tendencies, there was no way that I could continue to let him be my man. I decided that it would be best to just try and distance myself from him altogether for the simple fact that if word ever got out that he was homo, I couldn't take a chance on what the possible backlash of that could be to me and my club. The hard part was gonna be figuring out just how to go about distancing myself from him and his dominant ways.

It had been two weeks since I'd caught Tut with his dick

up Joystick's ass. And within those two weeks, I had two new problems that sprang up. One was that Destiny had escaped from prison, and the other thorn in my ass was that Brazil had pulled it off and opened up her new strip club called Magic City, and the buzz surrounding her club was ridiculous.

The ace in the hole that I had was Shabazz. I had spoken to him at length about all of my problems. Although I never enlightened him about Tut's gay tendencies, I did tell him that I needed for him to make Tut as well as some of my other two major headaches completely disappear.

For obvious reasons, Shabazz never felt comfortable talking over the phone, so he and I were planning on meeting to talk about exactly what it was that I needed for him to do for me. Basically I was gonna make him a financial offer, one that I knew he wouldn't refuse, to kill King Tut and to get the police to do whatever it was that they had to do to find and lock Destiny's ass back up. And, lastly, I needed him to work his connections so that they could harass Brazil and her new club until they were able to hit her with enough violations to shut her shit down.

So as I waited at the club for Shabazz to arrive on a Thursday afternoon, I baby-oiled my body and put on some sexy stripper shit that he liked. I knew that sex would precede every meeting that me and Shabazz had, and I wanted to do whatever I had to do to get him in the best of possible moods before this particular meeting simply because this would be the first time that I would ever ask him to kill someone for me.

The intercom began to buzz, and I quickly got up and trotted to the back door of the club. I opened the door and immediately tried to slam it shut when I realized that it was Tut at the door and not Shabazz.

Tut stuck his foot at the base of the thick black steel

door before it closed. "Bitch, open this fuckin' door!" Tut hollered as he pushed the door with much force.

"Tut, I told you I don't wanna see you. Move before I slam your fingers in this door," I shouted back. I desperately tried to push back on my side of the door with all of my might.

Unfortunately Tut's strength won out over mine, and he forced his way into the club. "Why the hell you change the locks?" Tut yelled. "And what the fuck you dressed like that for?"

"Tut, I changed the locks because I don't want certain people up in here! Didn't you see on the news that Destiny escaped from that prison bus?"

Tut looked at me with a screw face as his Hulk Hogan-looking chest heaved up and down.

"And you ain't my man no more, Tut. So don't question me about what the fuck I got on."

"Essence, you better start showing me more respect. And how the hell you gonna change the locks and not tell me? I stayed away from your ass for a minute to let you calm down, but don't get it twisted, I run this mutha-fucka!"

I threw my hands up in the air and then I walked to my office to go get my checkbook and a small lockbox that I had with wads of cash.

"Tut, look"—I held open the lockbox of cash for him to see—"How much you want? Just give me a figure. I'll write a check if I have to. I just want you out of *my* club and out of *my* life, period! The sex was good, what we had was good—*it was fake*—but it was good. But that shit is over, Tut. I gotta move on and that's it. I ain't gonna get into all that other shit."

Tut exhaled in anger and frustration, and just as he was about to say something, the intercom rang.

Gotdamn! I knew it was Shabazz, and that there was gonna be some shit, since Tut had seen the way I was dressed.

"Who dat?" Tut asked, pressing the talk button on the intercom.

There was a pause.

"I said who is it?" he yelled.

"It's Shabazz."

Tut looked at me as if he wanted an explanation.

"Tut, just buzz him in," I replied with an attitude as I walked toward the intercom box.

Tut just looked at me, so I bypassed him and pressed the button on the intercom to give Shabazz access to the club.

Shabazz yelled out to me, "Essence, you a'ight?"

"Essence, he coming to check for you?"

I walked out of my office to meet Shabazz and chat him up real quick. I was planning on just telling him to bounce and that I would get up with him later. I was sure that he would have been able to read between the lines, but before I could even properly greet him, Tut had beat me to the punch.

"What's the deal, homey? The club ain't open now. What's going on?" Tut asked in authoritative fashion, and didn't try to get a pound or anything from Shabazz.

Shabazz had on a pair of baggy dark blue Sean John jeans, his signature tan construction Timberlands, a green army fatigue jacket, and a black skullcap.

Shabazz looked at me, trying to figure out what was going on. He cautiously greeted Tut, extending his hand for a pound. "What up, my nigga?" Shabazz said.

Tut didn't respond to Shabazz. Instead he just turned and looked at me and stared me down. Then from out of nowhere, he slapped the shit outta me. *WHACK!*

"This nigga? Essence, you playing me for this chump-ass muthafucka!" Tut yelled at me.

I held on to the right side of my stinging face. My mouth felt like it was bleeding from the blow, but before I could check for blood, Shabazz pulled his gun from his waistband. "Tut, chill the fuck out!" Shabazz yelled as he ran up on Tut and pointed his gun square at Tut's face.

He'd caught Tut off guard, and Tut immediately backed up off of me and held his hands up in surrender. But I could tell from the smirk on Tut's face that he wasn't intimidated by Shabazz.

"You gonna pull a gun on my ass and you work for me? You crazy or what?" Tut asked.

"Essence, what you want me to do with this nigga? Just let me know now." Shabazz's face was full of nervous energy and intensity.

"Shabazz, put that burner away. Essence, go put some fuckin' clothes on." Tut turned and walked away from Shabazz, totally disrespecting his authority.

Shabazz approached Tut from behind with his gun still aimed at him, and as he walked, he looked over to me for direction on what I wanted him to do.

Tut must have had eyes in the back of his head or something, because as soon as Shabazz looked at me, he spun around and, with the hand speed of a heavyweight champion, knocked the gun out of Shabazz's hand, and with the same arm grabbed Shabazz and locked him in a chokehold.

Shabazz's gun had fallen to the floor and slammed up against the wall on the opposite side of the room. Tut then pulled his own gun from his waistband and put it to Shabazz's head while he kept him in the headlock with his other hand. Shabazz's back was to Tut's chest and Tut held him toward my direction so he could also keep an eye on me.

"Essence, tell him whatchu want him to do with me," Tut yelled at me, mocking Shabazz.

"Tut, just chill the fuck out," I said in a somewhat begging tone.

Tut looked as if he was applying serious pressure to Shabazz's throat, his muscular arm looking like a boa constrictor squeezing its prey. Shabazz was completely helpless, because if he'd tried to fight his way out, Tut woulda shot his ass in the back of the head.

Shabazz looked at me, his eyes looking like they were about to completely bulge out of their sockets from the pressure being applied to his throat.

Tut screamed, "You want me to chill the fuck out when this nigga just pulled a gun on me? Huh? Answer me." Tut took the skully off of Shabazz's head and flung it across the room.

"You fuckin' this nigga, right?" he asked me.

"No, Tut," I yelled back. My heart was racing, and I was sure that Tut was about to kill both me and Shabazz.

Tut yelled even louder, "Essence, don't lie to me. Are you fuckin' this nigga?"

I shook my head no and said no all at the same time.

Tut didn't immediately say anything in response. He clenched his teeth and pressed the gun into Shabazz's skull so hard, it was as if he was mushing Shabazz.

Shabazz grunted in fear and I was sure that he thought he was about to get shot.

Tut started to laugh at Shabazz's reaction. "Look at this nigga flinching and whining like a little bitch," Tut said as he continued to chuckle. "I tell you what"—Tut pulled Shabazz closer to him and kissed him on his right earlobe—"Since you flinching like a little bitch, why don't you be *my* bitch." He then proceeded to stick his tongue in Shabazz's ear.

"Uggggh!" Shabazz tried to yell as he feverishly began trying to free himself of Tut's grip.

"Ha, ha, ha, ha, ha!" Tut smacked Shabazz upside the head with the butt of the gun. "Calm the fuck down, nigga." Tut gave him another peck on the earlobe. "What? Essence ain't tell you how I get down?"

"Tut, a'ight, enough, enough! I asked you before, What the fuck do you want? Just tell me and I gotchu, and we go our separate ways! We ain't gotta go through all of this," I screamed.

When I was done talking, Tut whacked Shabazz upside the head with the butt of the gun, which dropped Shabazz to his knees. Then he whacked him upside the head again and proceeded to pistol-whip and kick him.

"Essence, this is *my* mutherfuckin' club, don't get it twisted. Where you went wrong is when you decided to stop fuckin' with a *real* man like me. You fuckin' wit' these bitch-ass niggas? The fuck is wrong wit'chu? I run this shit! Now get your muthafuckin' *little man* from up off of my floor. Leave those keys right there on that counter and, both of y'all, get the fuck out."

I went to Shabazz's aid. He was beyond woozy as he bled from the back of his head. I tried to get him to his feet, but I was having a hard time because of how heavy he felt.

"Hurry up with that pathetic nigga!" Tut barked.

Tut had definitely punked Shabazz in a way that I would have never envisioned. He showed who had the real power. Which reminded me as to exactly why I had always been drawn to him like a magnet from day one.

I had to do something, because my power was quickly evaporating, and I couldn't have that.

Chapter Fourteen

Destiny

I had remained in the boiler room of that apartment building for two and a half days straight. I had no watch, but I was able to keep track of time from the sunlight that shined through the one window. Although no one had come into the boiler room, and I hadn't heard any voices or footsteps outside of the room, I was still scared about venturing outside, not knowing what was lurking outside.

By the time the second day had arrived I figured that the manhunt for me would have had to have died down a bit, at least in that immediate area because the area was so large. I hadn't slept all that good and I was beyond hungry. I was also thirsty as hell. I had taken a shit and I had pissed twice in the corner on the opposite side of the room that I was hiding in. So in terms of relieving myself I was fine. I did need a shower in the worst way, but that was the least of my worries.

That Saturday afternoon I figured that I would wait until late that night before making my move for freedom. I wanted to make my move at three o'clock in the morning, but since I had no way of accurately knowing what time it was, I just had to make my best guess and then go for it.

After it had been dark for a good long while, I stood up and attempted to dust myself off the best I could with the handcuffs that I had on and slowly walked toward the boiler room door. The room was very dark, except for a glimmer from the street lamps outside.

When I reached the door, I put my ear to it and listened closely. When I didn't hear anything, I twisted the door-knob. My heart raced with extreme nervousness as I opened the door and veered out before venturing down pitch-black hallways.

I had no idea what direction I was walking in. Basically I had to walk very slowly and feel around with my hands like a blind person. I decided to just walk all the way to my left until I bumped into a wall. I figured that once I found a wall, I would just use my hands to feel along it and use it as a guide. At the same time I was hoping to find a light switch.

Two minutes into walking around in what felt like cir-cles, I finally felt something that felt like a light switch. I caressed and massaged it just to be sure that it was. It def-initely felt like one. I said a quick prayer and then just took a chance and flipped it and, thank God, a light came on. The light was bright as hell, and that actually caused me to panic more than walking in the dark. I surveyed the room and realized that I was right near the super's apart-ment. And no sooner than I had tiptoed past the super's apartment, I heard a dog barking and that scared the liv-ing shit outta me.

My instincts told me to just run straight for another door that I had seen, and that was exactly what I did. The barks from a large-sounding dog appeared to be coming

from the super's apartment. And although I was in no immediate danger of being bit by the dog, I didn't want the
dog's barking to cause the super or anyone else to get
suspicious.

The door that I had run into led me into another little
room, where I stayed stiff and frozen-still for a while, my
heart pounding. I waited about five minutes, until the dog
had stopped barking and my heart rate calmed down.
Again I felt for a light switch for like ten minutes until I
found one.

When the light came on, it turned out that I was in some
sort of utility room that had gas meters and electric meters everywhere. There were a bunch of porno magazines
on the wall and large-ass rattraps on the ground. The rattraps freaked me out, and I quickly decided to search
around the room to see if I could find an exit way that led
to the street or to another part of the building.

I didn't find an exit out of the building, but what I did
find was some dirty dark blue clothes that looked similar
to what a mechanic's uniform. The clothes were dirty as
hell, but to me, at that moment in time they looked like
Prada. I quickly searched through the clothes and found a
pair of pants and a shirt that were big enough to fit over
the orange jumpsuit I was wearing.

With the handcuffs on, it to took me a while to put on
the pants, but they were so long, I had to cuff them at the
bottom. Since I couldn't fit both of my arms into the long-
sleeve button-down shirt, I just draped the shirt around
my back and shoulders and let it hang like a cape and held
on to it with my hands.

After I left that utility room, I knew I had to hurry up
and find that door that I'd originally used to come into the
basement. Luckily, the light in the hallway was still on,
and within like two minutes I had found the door I was
looking for, and I walked out of the building.

The street was eerily quiet. I walked as fast as I could away from the busy Queens Boulevard and made it to a less quiet back street. I began to briskly walk toward Lefferts Boulevard.

When I made it to Lefferts, I decided to use a pay phone to call my homegirl Cathy collect. I was taking a serious chance in calling her because she had visited me in jail a couple of times, so I was worried that the cops might be watching her to see if I would in fact call her.

As the operator connected the call, I prayed that Cathy was home and would answer her phone. After four rings, a huge Kool-Aid smile came across my face when Cathy answered the phone.

"Hello, Cathy?"

"Yeah, who dis?" a tired-sounding Cathy asked.

"Cathy, it's me, Destiny. Cathy, I need you to wake up, wake up, wake up, wake up," I pleaded, whispering as loud as I could.

"Okay, I'm up. Where are you?"

"I don't know what's up with the phones, so I gotta talk really quick. I need you to come get me. I'm in Queens. I'm gonna be on the corner of Lefferts Boulevard and Hillside Avenue. Just act like you were going to Promiscuous Girl, but keep coming down Hillside in the direction of where the numbers get lower and you'll run into Lefferts Boulevard, okay?" I had to spell it out, since Cathy was from Washington Heights in Manhattan, which was about twenty-five minutes away from where I was at in Queens.

"Okay, I got you," Cathy said, sounding much more alert, like she had fully woken up. "I'ma be there."

I hung up the phone and hoped that the police hadn't tapped Cathy's phone. I headed down Lefferts Boulevard toward Hillside Avenue and hoped that Cathy would pick me up before anyone, especially the police, spotted me.

When Cathy had shown up and got me, we both agreed that me going back to her apartment wouldn't be smart, so she and I ended up going to a friend of ours named Stacey who danced at Sue's.

"Destiny, you are wild for the night!" Stacey joked as she warmed up some leftover Popeyes chicken for me to eat. "Shooting bitches in the street and escaping from prison buses? I thought you was always on that Kimora Lee diva shit."

I shook my head and lifted the bottle of Snapple Iced Tea to my mouth. "Things just kinda happened," I said, in a feeble attempt to explain my actions.

Cathy was looking in her cell phone when she asked Stacey if she had a number for Shabazz. "That nigga stay switching up his cell phones," Cathy added.

"Shabazz?" I asked.

Stacey confirmed that she had his number in her phone and she went to get it.

"Which Shabazz you talking about?" I asked, as Stacey returned with her phone and Shabazz's number.

"How many Shabazz do you know?" Cathy asked. "The one that work at your club, that Shabazz. I'ma get that nigga to come over here and get these cuffs off of you."

"What? You losing me."

Stacey blurted out, "Destiny, stop acting like you don't know that nigga's a cop?"

"*Shabazz*? Get the fuck outta here!"

Cathy and Stacey laughed at me because they thought I was bullshitting them.

"No, for real, is he?"

"Yes, I know you know that. He one of them grimy-ass cops. That's why I wanna call him, 'cause he'll take these cuffs off and won't trip. I mean, the nigga might want some pussy, wit' his sexy ass, but the hell." Cathy laughed.

"Yo, I swear to God, for as long as I knew Shabazz, I never knew he was five-O. When did he become a cop?"

"That nigga been a cop for a minute, but he keep the shit quiet 'cause he be busting cats on that deep cover shit, so he don't be wanting people to know." Stacey laughed. "You musta never gave that nigga no pussy, that's why."

"Nah, I mean he's cute and all, and he stay flirtin' with my ass, but y'all know me and how I get down. I ain't fuckin' wit' a dude unless he ballin' for real. A nigga got to pay for this pussy, and my shit don't come cheap."

Stacey said, "Trust me, Destiny, that nigga is getting that money. He be robbing niggas and shit."

Cathy couldn't get in touch with Shabazz, so she left him a message asking him to call her as soon as possible.

By that time it was nearing five o'clock in the morning, and Cathy decided that she would just crash at Stacey's crib, which was in the East New York section of Brooklyn, instead of driving all the way back to Manhattan. The two of them got a knife and a pair of scissors and they helped cut me out of that prison jumpsuit that I was still wearing. And Stacey gave me a spare robe and some of her clothes to put on and pointed me in the direction of her bathroom.

There, I took one of the best and most needed showers of my life. When I was done showering, I decided to just keep on the terry cloth robe and sleep in that, figuring I would put on the clothes that Stacey had given me after I woke up.

I came into the living room and found Stacey and Cathy both smoking weed.

"You wanna hit this?" Stacey asked.

"Oh, you ain't say nothing but a word!" I eagerly took the blunt from her and inhaled like my life depended on it.

Stacey then cracked open three bottles of Corona, and we each started to drink from a bottle.

In about five minutes, my head was buzzing and I was feeling nice. Finally after all that stress that I had been through with jail and all that drama I was able to relax and unwind for just a bit. Although the weed and the beer made me feel good, I was still horny as hell, considering that I hadn't had sex in months.

"*Mwah!*" I kissed Stacey on the cheek to thank her. "Thank you, ma."

"What about me? I don't get no love?"

"Oh, I'm sorry, boo." I leaned over and kissed Cathy right on her lips and waited for a reaction from her.

She smiled. I knew that we both we feeling real nice at that point. Without saying anything, Cathy leaned toward me again, and we both began tongue-kissing each other. I'd had lesbian experiences before, so it was nothing to me. And I was sure that both Cathy and Stacey had as well.

Before I could blink, my robe was off and I was butt naked and with my legs spread wide open. Stacey was alternating between sucking on my nipples and tongue-kissing me, while Cathy worked her tongue on my clit, sliding her finger in and out of my pussy.

Cathy had a magical tongue.

I held on to her soft, long hair and worked my hips as she inserted another finger into my pussy. "Oh God, you're gonna make me cum!" I thrust my pussy into Cathy's face and came harder than I ever did in my life.

"Whooo! Whoo! I needed that real bad," I said, my chest heaving up and down from breathing so hard.

But I couldn't be selfish. I had to return the favor.

Cathy and Stacey both quickly undressed, and Cathy was soon sitting on my face as I lay on my back on Stacey's living room floor. And while I ate Cathy out, she was eating out Stacey.

My pussy was so wet and I was so turned-on that I had

to stick my finger inside of my pussy and massage my clit, handcuffs and all, until I came a second time.

After we all came, we were all feeling so good that we didn't wanna move, and we fell asleep right there on the living room floor.

When I woke up I found myself on Stacey's bed. I must have been so tired and knocked out, because I didn't remember ever getting in her bed.

"Wake up wit' yo sexy ass!" Shabazz playfully said to me as he shook me and woke me up.

"Hey, baby. What's up?" I said through my grogginess. I sat up in the bed and tried to gather myself. My titties were fully exposed, and the rest of my butt-naked body was underneath the covers.

"Let me get your wrists." Shabazz took hold of the handcuffs and unlocked them.

Shabazz and I had never really been close. We had conversations before, but we were never really on a cool basis outside of the strip club. At that moment, though, he was my best friend. I reached up and wrapped my arms around his neck and pulled him on to the bed and kissed him on his cheeks.

"Thank you!" I hollered. "You are a lifesaver. And how come I'm just finding out you a cop?" I playfully punched Shabazz in the arm.

"You better watch yourself, pulling me on top of you like that, getting a nigga's dick all hard and shit."

I was no dummy. Realizing the predicament I was in, I knew the benefits that Shabazz could bring me, so I quickly grabbed hold of him even tighter. I whispered to him, "That dick feels good too. I feel it pressing on my leg."

I knew that I had Shabazz wide open. If giving that nigga some pussy was all it would take for him to help me out a little and look out for me, then that wasn't gonna be a problem. For about the half an hour that Shabazz hung out at Stacey's house, I walked around naked the entire time. I knew that he was strictly thinking with his dick, and that was exactly what I wanted him to do. In less than an hour I had him asking me if I wanted to come back with him to chill at his crib.

"Yeah, no doubt," I replied nonchalantly, but inside I was cheesing to no end.

Chapter Fifteen

Brazil

Promiscuous Girl was definitely the hottest strip club in New York. There was no question about that. Everything about that club was fire. From the celebrities who frequented the place, to the décor of the club, to the sexy dancers, it had it all. But what had really gotten Promiscuous Girl over for all the years that it had been on top was the fact that it was also an underground haven for drugs and prostitution.

With Magic City, I knew that I wouldn't immediately be able to have the hot décor that Promiscuous Girl had, and while I had masterminded the entire Promiscuous Girl prostitution hustle by bringing girls back and forth from the country of Brazil to work as prostitutes, I had no plans on having Magic City be a front for drugs and prostitution. Although the drugs and prostitution brought in boatloads of money, it also attracted a shitload of drama and an element that I didn't want associated with my spot.

Getting sexy dancers wasn't going to be a problem, so I knew that Magic City was going to outshine Promiscuous Girl, since I was going to be relentless in promoting the club. And unlike Promiscuous Girl, where we used to be so preoccupied with the male celebrities who showed up at the club on a regular basis, I wanted to attract female stars and females with relevant brand names to come out to the club, to separate Magic City. If I did that and got the word out that those female stars would be in attendance, then I knew that the men would flock to my new strip club.

My plan worked like a charm. I had shelled out ten thousand dollars to get Buffie The Body to make an appearance on opening night, and another fifteen thousand dollars to get DJ Funkmaster Flex. Flex had promoted my spot all week long while he deejayed on the radio. Through her website and through her MySpace page, Buffie The Body promoted that she would be appearing at Magic City and signing copies of her new swimsuit calendar. I had also gotten the word out through flyers and I even placed a quarter-page ad in the *Daily News*. I had also personally reached out to everybody I knew, telling them to come out to my new spot. And I also had security in place, so that no bullshit would pop off.

On the opening night, Magic City went bananas. It was an absolute zoo! So many people showed up to the spot that we had to turn people away at the door. Aside from celebrities who wanted to get in, once the club was filled to capacity, the only exceptions that we were making was, in addition to the twenty-dollar cover charge, if people were willing to buy a bottle of liquor for upwards of two hundred and fifty dollars a bottle, then and only then would we let them inside the club. Since all of the fellas wanted to get in and get close to Buffie, a good majority of people were going in their wallets and shelling out that money.

Funkmaster Flex shouted into the mic, "Shout out to my girl Brazil in the house looking real sexy! I see you, ma. You a survivor, ya hearrrrd!" Then he threw on the hit Lost Boyz record, "Lights, Camera, Action!"

"Brazil, you killing 'em wit' that tattoo!"

Funkmaster Flex was referring to this brand-new tattoo I had of a black panther that ran from my back and wrapped around to my stomach and gave the appearance that the panther was climbing my body. I'd got the tattoo to cover up the scars that the bullet wounds had left on my body.

Although all of my weight had not yet returned and I tired easily, my body still looked hot. I showed it off with this black Calvin Klein tube top that was held up by a gold snake chain that wrapped around my neck. I also had on some black pants and some gold high-heel shoes.

My doctor told me that he didn't want me drinking and that I needed to get as much rest as possible, but those instructions went out the window as I drank glass after glass of liquor and partied and mingled with everybody until the wee hours of Friday morning.

"Shout out to Buffie The Body in the house," Funkmaster Flex shouted over the mic. "Mr. Cheeks, Tony Yayo, I see you, kid!"

"Brazil, this placed is rammed!" Vegas yelled into my ear over the loud music.

"That's what the fuck I'm talking about," I yelled back. Then I asked him was everything all right on the security end, and he told me that security was holding it down.

"Walk around and make sure everybody is spending money," I shouted into his ear, before walking off to go take photos with Buffie and some of the other celebrities who were in the house.

As I walked past this dancer named Tiffany, one of the many Promiscuous Girl dancers I had recruited to come dance at Magic City, she said to me, "Brazil, this is the new spot. You know you 'bout to shut Essence the fuck down, right?"

"Did I lie to you?" I asked her. "You better go get that money." I smiled and playfully tapped her on her ass.

"Fellas," Funkmaster Flex shouted, "next Thursday, Vida Guerra will be in the house." Then he played his signature sound of an exploding bomb.

With the tons of money that I had made that night and with all of the fun that I was having, the biggest satisfaction that I got was in knowing that I had made it through Destiny and Essence's hate. They both would have died with hate, had they seen me living it up and basking in my glory.

I held my bottle of Hennessy up in the air as I walked through my club gloating my ass off. Right on cue, as if Funkmaster Flex was able to read my mind, he threw on 50 Cent's record, "Hate It or Love It".

The chorus to the song was so on point, I shouted the lyrics into the air.

Chapter Sixteen

Essence

I had driven past Brazil's club at eleven PM on the first night that it opened and I must admit that a smile came across my face as I slowly nodded and looked at the chaotic scene of cars and people in front of her club. The bitch had pulled it off. What else could I say?

Immediately I dialed Shabazz's cell phone, and it rang out to voice mail like it had been doing ever since yesterday afternoon after Tut had punked him in my club.

"Shabazz, I need you to call me back. I been leaving you messages. Call me back, let me know what's good wit'chu."

I knew that Shabazz's pride and his ego had both been destroyed, and that was more than likely the reason why he was avoiding me. But, as far as I was concerned, he needed to hurry up and get over that shit with Tut so he could help me to get Brazil's club shut down. I didn't have time for him to be getting all sensitive on me and shit. And if he was gonna get all sensitive, then what he should have done was fought Tut back like a man, even if it meant that Tut woulda popped a cap in his head.

After staking out Magic City for about an hour, I decided to drive off and head home. As I drove, I called Shabazz two more times and still I got no answer from him. I was really starting to get pissed off with him.

Call his ass one more time and if he don't pick up, then don't fuck with that nigga no more, I told myself as I walked into my house and put my keys on top of my kitchen counter and began to pour myself some Alizé.

I gulped down the glass of Alizé and then dialed Shabazz from my home phone. I was hoping that he wouldn't recognize the number and I would catch him off guard, but his phone went to voice mail again.

Shit! I screamed in my head.

"You know what? Shabazz, this shit is fuckin' ridiculous! I been calling you and calling you, and you and I know you see my number poppin' up on your phone and you playing me for a fool. I needed you to help me with this issue with Brazil, but obviously your punk ass is still buggin' the fuck out over that shit yesterday. And, you know what, I realize now that you are a fuckin' pussy. You ain't nothing but a bitch, just like Tut said you was, corny muthafucka!" And for extra emphasis, I shouted, "Fuckin' clown!" Then I hung up the phone.

I had a screw face on as I headed straight to my living room and turned on the TV and practically drank myself into a coma as I tried to figure out what my next move should be.

Chapter Seventeen

[One hour after leaving Stacey's house with Shabazz]

Destiny

Shabazz lived in White Plains, which was in Westchester County, not too far from the Bronx. He lived on the twelfth floor of a nice high-rise condominium building that had a doorman, a swimming pool, a gym, and the whole nine yards.

"Shabazz, your spot is off the damn chain," I said to him as we entered his immaculate apartment.

"Yeah, it's cool. I been here for a minute now. I'm thinking about getting a crib out on Long Island or maybe even moving to New Jersey," he said as he took me on a quick tour of the two-bedroom apartment.

We eventually ended up sitting on his living room couch, where he explained to me exactly how serious a risk he was taking by chilling with me.

"If *anything* goes down, I need you to swear on your life that you say that you never knew that I was a cop and that I never knew that you was on the run, a'ight?"

"No doubt."

"I mean, we should be a'ight, but I'm just saying, you never know."

"Nah, believe me, I totally understand. I mean, I am just so thankful that you could look out for me like this."

"It's nothing, but what you should do is cut your hair off and dye that shit a different color. And, whatever you do, don't drive unless you're with me, 'cause if we get stopped by the police, all I gotta do is flash my badge and we'll be good."

I nodded my head, and then Shabazz asked me if I wanted anything to drink, but I wasn't thirsty, so I said no.

"Let me use your bathroom real quick," I said as I got up from the couch and walked to the bathroom to pee. I knew where the bathroom was at because of the quick tour that he'd just taken me on.

After I peed and wiped myself and washed my hands and came back to the living room, Shabazz was sitting on his couch butt-ass naked.

"*Okay.*" I smiled and stood still in my tracks.

Shabazz motioned for me to come sit down next to him, so I did. He began stroking his dick and leaned over and started kissing me. I knew what time it was. I knew that sex was gonna be part of the arrangement, so I just went with the flow.

When we were done kissing, I grabbed his rock-hard dick and got down on my knees and started sucking on it. I alternated between deep-throating his dick and stroking the shaft with my right hand. In between, I would spit on his dick to keep it lubricated. If there was one thing that I was good at, it was sucking dick. I had more skills than Superhead. That probably was because since the age of twelve I started sneaking to have sex with my older cousin and had a lot of time to work on my skills.

"Ah, yeah, that shit feels good. Suck that dick, baby," Shabazz said to me.

As usual whenever I sucked dick, I would get turned on. My pussy was pulsating, so I started to rub on it.

"Take your clothes off."

I wiped my mouth and smiled. Then I stood up and started to get undressed. "You got a condom, baby?"

He looked good, but I had no idea where his dick had been. And, besides, he had no idea who I'd been with.

Shabazz shook his head. "I don't think so." Then he walked off to his room, saying he would be right back. He came back without the condom. "I must have ran out."

Granted, I looked good but, just like Tut and all the rest of the niggas who I fucked wit', Shabazz had no idea who I'd been with or if I had any type of diseases. Yet, he was ready and willing to run up in me raw.

"How you want it?" I asked.

Shabazz sat down on the couch and told me he wanted me on top.

So with my chest facing him, I straddled him, while he guided his dick into my wet, pulsating pussy. I held on to the headrest of his couch so I could get some leverage, and I began riding his dick like a porno star. I was definitely trying to please him, and at the same time, I was working my hips and ass so that I could cum. His dick felt good as hell.

"I ain't had no dick in a minute," I said, breathing really heavy. I could tell that I was about to cum.

"You a fuckin' fantasy." Shabazz held on to my back and stood up, his dick still inside my pussy.

I wrapped my arms around his neck and my legs around his waist. I didn't realize that he was so strong as he lifted me up and down on his dick. It felt so good. I couldn't help it and I hollered as I came. I knew that all of his neighbors were probably shocked at the sounds that I was making on a Sunday afternoon, but I didn't care. I was always uninhibited whenever I had sex.

After I came, Shabazz slid his dick out of me and guided me back to the couch. Then he asked me to turn around so that he could fuck me from behind. I did as he said, and within seconds he had his dick back inside of me and was humping me faster than a jackrabbit. I reached my hand between my legs so that I could feel his balls while they smacked up against my ass, and after about a minute or so of rubbing on his balls, I could tell that he was getting reading to cum.

"Don't cum inside of me, okay, baby?" I panted.

Shabazz said okay, but he didn't listen to me and he came all up in my pussy. My first instinct was to get upset with him for bussing inside of me, but the sex was so good that I let it slide.

I turned around and asked him if it was good.

"Hell fuckin' yeah, that shit was good." He smiled and tried to catch his breath. "I told you that you're a fantasy. I mean that shit."

I laughed. My body was still feeling nice and tingly, and I could feel Shabazz slide his dick out of me. "We can have round two tonight when you get off of work." I kissed him on his cheek before walking off to his bathroom to clean myself and freshen up.

"Fuck around and I'ma marry yo' ass," Shabazz joked.

[Almost two weeks later . . . still hiding out at Shabazz's crib]

Sex with Shabazz was good because it was new. And most new sex is good because it's usually not monotonous and boring. But while it was good, it seemed like I had woken up a monster or something. Shabazz literally wanted to have sex with me like three and four times a day. It was all good. I mean, his dick wasn't so big that it hurt me or anything, but my pussy was starting to get sore from all of the fucking that we were doing.

The way I looked at it, if it came down to me having to choose between a sore pussy because of too much sex or being locked up behind bars, I was gonna tolerate my sore pussy, because there was no way that I wanted to be locked up again.

Somehow, when Shabazz wasn't working and when we weren't fucking, I found time to take care of my hair. I had decided to just go to a beauty parlor that Stacey had recommended to me. I felt safe, since Shabazz escorted me. I ended up cutting my long hair into one of those early nineties short Halle Berry styles. And I dyed my hair brown and added some red highlights to it, all of which Shabazz put up the money for.

Even if someone really knew me, unless they stared at me, they wouldn't have immediately recognized me. So that brought me a great sense of relief. But I couldn't rest on a change in hairstyle alone. I also had to scale down the way I dressed so that I didn't attract too much attention to myself.

Going back to my apartment, or even trying to contact any of my relatives would have been way too risky and out of the question, so there was no way I could have retrieved any of my old clothes. Thankfully, though, Shabazz looked out and bought me five brand-new outfits to rock, along with new shoes and sneakers.

The arrangement that he and I had was good, but I knew that I was really vulnerable because, if the sex ever got whack to him or if he ever got tired of me or if the cops got wind of the fact that he was housing an escapee, I would have been left up shit's creek to dry. For the time being though, I had to just deal with it, until I could figure out just exactly what I needed to do to make things happen for myself.

For the first week and a half that I had been shacking up with him, I made sure that I cooked and cleaned for him and made him feel like a king, and I never questioned him about anything, so that I wouldn't fuck up and say the wrong thing.

Then late one Wednesday, at like seven thirty in the evening or so, Shabazz came home, his face fucked-up like he had been in a fight. There was blood on his shirt and he was very heated.

"Baby, what happened? Are you okay?" I asked out of real, genuine concern. Shabazz was supposed to be at work with the NYPD, or at least that's what I thought, so immediately I figured that something must have happened while he was on the job.

"That nigga Tut is dying tonight!" Shabazz said as he went into his closet and unlocked a metal box and took out two guns and threw them on the bed, along with two clips of ammunition.

"Shabazz, what happened?" I asked, desperately wanting to know what was going on.

"The less you know, the better." He put the clips into the guns and prepared to leave.

"Shabazz, look at your face. At least let me clean your face up for you," I pleaded, hoping he would listen to me.

Shabazz paused for a second and angrily bit on his bottom lip. His cell phone began buzzing, and he answered it.

"Yeah . . . in Queens, off Hillside Avenue," Shabazz stated to whoever he was talking to. Then he added, "Nah, I don't know where the nigga live at. . . . You can't get there any sooner?" he asked. "A'ight, so at ten o'clock. One." He then hung up the phone.

"Hugggghh!" He yelled and punched a huge hole into his living room wall in the process.

From what I could decipher, something had gone down between Shabazz and King Tut, so I took the liberty and just assumed that I knew what his phone conversation was about. "Shabazz, if you wanna know where Tut lives at, I know where he lives. He lives on Long Street in Southside. Over near Baisley projects."

Shabazz looked at me. "You sure you know where the nigga live at? Like you know the exact house and everything?"

"Yes, I know the exact house and all that."

"A'ight, good. Here's the deal."

Shabazz went on to explain to me how Essence had King Tut and two of his boys pistol-whip him.

"But for what?" I asked, trying to make sense of everything. I knew Essence was a snake-ass bitch who was only worried about herself, so the truth of the matter was that nothing concerning her and some petty beef surprised me anymore. And that's what I explained to Shabazz as I tended to his wounds.

Shabazz then went to ask me if I could help him to set up King Tut. Before I could answer him, he got up from the chair I had him sitting in while I tended to his cuts and he said, "Destiny, I gotta be straight-up with you about something."

Again before I could reply to him he took the liberty to speak before I spoke and he went on to explain and confirm for me just what I had been thinking about when I was in prison. Essence and King Tut had orchestrated the whole snitching drama with Brazil simply so they could get me to take out Brazil and then take the fall for the whole shit in the process.

Part of me listened in disbelief as Shabazz spoke, part of me was angry, and part of me was confused. I didn't know what the fuck to think, simply because everybody seemed like they were lying. However, I knew that Shabazz, if he was lying, had the most to lose because he was a gotdamn cop. So why the hell would he be lying?

I thought to myself for a few minutes before making my intentions known to Shabazz that I would in fact help him set up King Tut and his phony bullshit ass.

"Baby, I gotchu on this," I said to him. "And I know exactly how to get at this nigga. I'm ready to do this when you are."

Chapter Eighteen

Brazil

After Buffie The Body made her appearance at Magic City on opening night and Vida Guerra made her appearance the following week, word spread like wildfire throughout New York, New Jersey, and Connecticut that Magic City was the place to be on Thursday nights.

In two weeks the club's success had far exceeded my expectations but I knew that I couldn't rest and get comfortable. If anything, I felt like I had to go harder at promoting my club so that we wouldn't lose the momentum that we had. And, thanks to a connection that Vegas had, we were able to get the former porn star Heather Hunter to agree to come to Magic City to make an appearance and to promote her new mix-tape.

We promoted the Heather Hunter appearance by letting everyone know that the cost to get in the club that night would be fifty dollars, but that would include an autographed copy of Heather Hunter's mix-tape as well as one picture with her.

I could tell that we were gonna make all kinds of money that night because most strip clubs don't really get poppin' until after midnight. But by nine o'clock the club was already rammed with people, and there was a huge line to get in. Funkmaster Flex wasn't available to do the music, so we got the legendary DJ Kid Capri to do the music and Kid Capri kept the whole atmosphere charged.

Heather Hunter's people had called to let us know that she was running behind schedule and that she wouldn't be arriving until about eleven thirty PM. That was cool as far as I was concerned because it gave people more time to spend money at the bar. Plus, I knew that Heather Hunter would definitely show up because there was no way that she would miss out on a $15,000 payday.

"Brazil to the front door, ma," Kid Capri shouted into the mic as he played the music.

At first I wasn't sure exactly what he was talking about, until one of the bouncers came up to me and explained what was going on.

"Brazil, Essence is at the door talking shit. You want us to let her in or what?" the bouncer who went by the name of OZ asked me.

"Hell fuckin' no," I screamed over the loud music. "Y'all know what I said about that bitch. I don't want her ass or Destiny up in my muthafuckin' club." I headed toward the front door with OZ.

OZ and I slowly made our way through the throngs of people, and my pressure was raising by the second. I was ready for war by the time I reached the front door.

"Brazil, it's like that?" Essence asked me as she stood looking like a million dollars in her black high-heel, over-the-knee Bottega Veneta boots along with a Stella McCartney cashmere shawl cardigan? and a Stella McCartney liquid jersey dress. "I ain't even allowed up in your spot? You fuckin' got me on a watch list and shit?" She turned to her two friends and chuckled. She was with some big fat butch-looking chick who was rocking a dude-like Caesar haircut. The other girl was slim and dressed in sneakers and jeans and she had her hair pulled back into a ponytail.

I will fuck all of these bitches up! I thought to myself, sensing that Essence had brought the two chicks with her so that they could help her fight her battles.

It was approaching eleven o'clock, and although I was pissed off I had to maintain my self-control because I knew that if I set off some shit and the cops came and shut the club down before Heather Hunter got there, I would've had a mess on my hands with the people who had already paid their money to get in. And there was a huge line of people still waiting to get in, and I wasn't trying to miss out on all of that money.

"Essence, this ain't Promiscuous Girl. I run this muthafucka, and I don't want your ass up in here!" I walked right up to her and stared her down and let her know that she wasn't intimidating me.

"Bitch, you stole my gotdamn money to open this muthafuckin' club, and you stole my dancers, and I can't even come up in here and get a drink?" Essence sarcastically asked. "Brazil, there's rules to this shit—"

WHAM!

Before Essence could finish talking, Vegas had emerged from within the crowd that had formed in front of the club and punched the shit out of Essence, knocking her ass right to the fucking ground.

"Buss her ass, Brazil!" someone yelled.

I couldn't pass up the opportunity and I instantly started stomping on Essence with all of the force I could muster up. Vegas must have knocked her ass out cold because Essence was on the concrete and barely moving while I stomped on her.

"You can't be hitting on my girl like that," the butch-looking chick screamed as she pushed me out of the way and attended to Essence, trying to pick her up off the ground.

Before I could blink there was straight chaos out in front of the club. OZ grabbed me and told me that he was taking me inside the club.

"Nah, get off me. I'ma fuck all these bitches up!" I said. At that point I had completely lost my temper and I didn't care about anything. I was seeing red and was ready to bring it to Essence and her little crew.

"Let that bitch go," the girl who was wearing the sneakers and jeans said to OZ, her hands raised like a boxer.

Pap, pap, pap, pap!

Those were the sounds that I heard. I immediately knew that it was gunshots coming from a small gun, probably a .22.

When OZ heard the shots he threw me to the ground and lay on top of me and started to yell for everybody to get down. "Get down, get down!"

OZ was so big and heavy that he was practically smothering me, and I couldn't see shit that was going on. From my position on the concrete the only thing that I could see were people's feet running past me and scrambling for cover.

After about thirty seconds or so OZ scooped me up off the ground and quickly hustled me inside the club and slammed the door behind us.

"OZ, you a'ight?" one of the other bouncers asked.

"Yeah, yeah, I'm good," OZ said, breathing real heavy. "Keep the doors closed. Ain't nobody coming in or out. Keep them shits closed."

"Yo, where's Vegas?" I asked, concern in my voice.

Everyone looked around and we didn't see Vegas, so I insisted that OZ open up the door, just in case Vegas was still trying to get inside.

"Brazil, they still shooting out there," OZ said.

"*Exactly*! Now open up the fuckin' door," I barked.

OZ complied with my wishes, and no sooner than he

had opened up the door, I could see cop cars coming from every direction. The cops began to throw everybody on the ground and up against the wall, and some cops ran inside the club.

In a matter of seconds the music had stopped and I was on the ground getting frisked by the police.

I was so angry as I lay on the ground that I felt like I was foaming at the mouth like a wild dog. Essence had managed to fuck up what would have been one of the best nights ever for Magic City. And I was sure that, with the violence and the fact that people had never gotten to see Heather Hunter, Magic City was gonna have a black eye that it would have to somehow recover from.

Chapter Nineteen

Essence

It had been close to a week since Vegas had caught me with a punch that knocked me out and bruised my face. But how whack is that for some nigga who's supposed to be so gangsta to be hitting a woman? Vegas is pussy. He knows it and I know it. I was gonna make sure that his ass got touched, but for the time being I had more important shit to concern myself with than Vegas and Brazil and her little club.

For one, I had been repeatedly calling King Tut and leaving him messages, but he wasn't getting back to me. His car was at his crib, but he wasn't inside his crib, and his mail was starting to pile up in his mailbox. None of his boys had seen or heard from him in a few days, and I was starting to get extremely worried. But when he didn't show up to Promiscuous Girl on Wednesday, I knew that something wasn't right.

The other problem that I had was that Shabazz was still on that bitch shit and still wasn't taking my calls or getting back to me, and by this point I had left him like a million messages. I had even called the police precinct that he worked out of and left a message for him there to get back to me, and he hadn't. I didn't know what to think or what was going on.

So Wednesday night going into Thursday morning after the club had closed, I decided to drive out to White Plains to Shabazz's apartment to see what was up with him. It was five o'clock in the morning, and I was tired as hell while I drove. But I didn't care because everything around me was starting to fall apart and I needed some answers.

At five thirty I reached Shabazz's building and I double-parked my car in the front of the building and walked into the lobby.

"Yeah, I'm here for twelve D," I said to the doorman, who was seated behind a fancy desk.

"Okay, just a minute," he said while he picked up a phone and punched in Shabazz's intercom number.

"Huh, yes sir, good morning. You have a visitor here to see you—Young lady, what is your name?"

"Essence. Tell him that Essence is here to see him," I replied.

The doorman relayed my information, and then he paused for a moment and nodded his head and said, "Okay." He hung up the phone and directed his attention toward me.

"Okay, Misss, you can take that elevator over there to your lift and go right up."

"Thank you," I said, a smile plastered across my face. I sashayed my way to the elevator and up to see Shabazz so I could handle my business. I was hoping that the nigga didn't want no early-morning pussy because I wasn't in the mood for that, nor was I there to do anything but discuss business.

Chapter Twenty

Destiny

"Tut, this is me, Destiny. I know you don't answer blocked numbers, but I can only call you from this number. I'm gonna call you back in like ten minutes, but I need you to pick up the phone. I know you know my situation. Pick up," I said in an urgent tone as I left a message for Tut on his cell phone.

"He'll pick up when I call him back," I said to Shabazz and his homeboy Jason, who was also a cop.

We were sitting in Shabazz's car on the corner of Merrick and Baisley, which was about two minutes away from Tut's house. It was just past ten o'clock at night.

After ten minutes had passed I called Tut's cell phone again, and it rang three times before he picked up.

"Yo," Tut said into the phone.

"Tut, what's up?" I asked, sounding excited to hear his voice.

"What's good, ma?" he asked with his deep-ass voice.

"Tut, look, you know I'm in some shit right now, and I really need your help."

/

"Destiny, we family, you know that. What's up? You know I got you."

"I need to crash for just one night, but I really need some dough. I wanna go down to Atlanta and lay low for a minute, but I don't have no money. Like, for real, for real, my pockets is on empty."

Tut told me that he would look out for me and that I could stay with him.

"But, Tut, listen, I need you to keep your mouth closed about speaking to me or seeing me, okay?'

"Destiny, you know me. What the fuck?"

I proceeded to tell Tut where I was at and that I needed him to come scoop me up. He explained to me that he was on the Van Wyck Expressway, coming back from Manhattan, and that he would be there to get me in about fifteen minutes. So with that I exited Shabazz's car and I waited near the side of an H&R Block store and hoped that no one would recognize me, especially considering that the 113th police precinct was right down the block.

Shabazz and his boy stayed in their car, but they parked across the street where they would be in full view of me. The plan was that after Tut picked me up and took me back to his house that they would follow him in their car.

Just as planned, Tut came pulling up to the corner fifteen minutes later and he looked around while I approached the car.

"Open the door," I said as I smiled and tapped on the window.

"Destiny?" Tut asked as he unlocked the power-locked doors. "Ohhh shit, you look different."

I climbed into his truck and I leaned over and gave him a kiss on the cheek. "I'm on the run, so I had to switch up my look."

"Wowww! I mean you still look good and all, don't get it

twisted. You just look different," he explained as he pulled off and headed toward his house.

I ran my hand down my face and I sighed and exhaled at the same time. "Tut, you don't even know the half of what I been through. Shit is crazy for me."

"Nah, I could imagine. But you'll be a'ight," he said as he turned on to his block. Then he asked me if I wanted something to eat.

"I'm good. Thanks for asking, though."

"Yeah, when we get in the crib you gotta fill me in on everything." Tut parked his car in front of his house, turned off the ignition, and exited the truck.

He got out on the driver's side, and I got out on the passenger's side. My heart was beating fast because I knew what was about to go down.

"If you even breathe, I'll blow your fuckin' brains out," Shabazz said as he ran up to Tut and put his 9 mm to his head.

Shabazz had a black S550 Mercedes Benz with dark tinted windows. Jason was driving the Benz and he was behind the wheel as he pulled right up near Tut's driveway. Shabazz forced Tut to walk toward the Benz and pushed him in the backseat at gunpoint. I got in the passenger seat, and Jason drove off and headed for the Van Wyck Expressway.

"Destiny, you still on that snake shit," Tut said to me as we drove off.

Blaow, blaow, blaow, blaow, blaow!

That was the deafening sound that I heard coming from the backseat.

"Oh shit!" Jason yelled as he turned and looked in the backseat and saw Tut's limp body and blood splattered all over the seats and rear windows. "I thought you was gonna wait until we got to the yard."

"Man, fuck this nigga!" Shabazz yelled. He was so angry that he started dumping more bullets into Tut's body.

I had no idea that Shabazz was so gangsta and could be so brutal, but I was even more surprised that he was so enraged.

After he was done firing his gun he spit in Tut's face. "Bitch-ass homo muthafucka!" he hollered.

Wow! I thought to myself. Although Tut had did me real dirty, we had had a connection. At least I did, based on all the sex he and I had had, so I did feel some remorse seeing him shot up and dead in the back of Shabazz's car the way he was. But in spite of feelings of remorse, I knew that Tut knew the way of the street, so he had to know that the consequences of crossing people could, and very often did, lead to death. And in his case it was his double-crossing snake-ass ways that had cost him his life, so I could only feel sorry for him but so much.

The mood inside the car was tense but eerily quiet as we navigated toward the Bronx. I didn't know what to say, but I wanted to say something to break the silence.

"Shabazz, you a damn beast!" I said as a compliment, a smile on my face.

Shabazz just looked at me and he didn't respond.

A part of me got nervous and started thinking crazy thoughts. Like outta nowhere, I started wondering if Shabazz had plans on killing me as well. I reclined in my seat and tried to relax and just waited for us to arrive where we were going.

After about twenty more minutes of driving we reached the Hunts Point section of the Bronx and maneuvered our way to this parking lot that had a bunch of trucks from a tree cutting company. And from what I could decipher from the limited talking between Jason and Shabazz, Jason's father owned the tree cutting company and that was how he had access to the lot.

Jason pulled up right behind this huge truck with a large opening in the back of it along with some machinery that was attached to it, and inside of the covered pick-up section of the truck was all kinds of chopped tree limbs, leaves, and shredded wood from trees that had been cut. The parking lot was dark, the only light coming from the surrounding streetlights and the headlights from Shabazz's car.

"Yo, that's the Chipper right there. I'ma start up the truck, and we'll be in and out in a few minutes." Jason exited the car and made his way to the front of the truck.

Shabazz also exited the Benz. It felt kinda spooky being in the car with Tut's dead body, so I also exited the car.

And just as I got out of the car the truck's engine started revving. Jason came walking briskly to the back of the truck and pressed some buttons on the back of the Chipper and it started to make this whirring sound, like a large fan.

"Grab that nigga and I'll help you lift his ass up," Jason said to Shabazz.

Shabazz quickly opened the rear passenger door of the Benz and grabbed a hold of Tut by reaching under his underarms and he pulled his body outta the car. Jason grabbed Tut's ankles while Shabazz still held on to him by the underarms.

"Damn, this muthafucka is heavy," Jason blurted out.

"It's all dead weight, that's why."

"Yo, on three we just gotta heave this muthafucka face first into them blades right there," Jason said to Shabazz.

Shabazz nodded his head.

Jason began his count, "One, two, three . . ."

"Huggh," Shabazz grunted as he and Jason hoisted Tut's body and threw it into the Chipper.

Jason held on to Tut's legs and sort of guided his body as it literally was shredded to nothing but red bloody pulp.

"Zzzzzzzzst," that was the sound that I repeatedly heard

as Tut's body literally disappeared into thin air as it went through the front of the Chipper like it was a tree limb and came out of the other end like a squished tomato.

"Yo, this the best invention they ever made." Shabazz began laughing and gave Jason a pound.

Jason trotted off and grabbed hold of a rake and with the rake he reached into the back of pick-up cabin of the Chipper and raked the mulch that was already in there so that it could mix with Tut's blood until you could no longer see any blood.

"This nigga just disappeared forever." Jason laughed and chucked the rake over into a corner.

And just like that, King Tut's reign had ended forever.

Me, Jason, and Shabazz headed back to Queens so that Jason could get his car, and then we went our separate ways. Shabazz and I headed back toward the Bronx, and Jason headed off on his own.

Shabazz leaned over and kissed me at the first red light that we came to. "Mission accomplished, baby," he said to me.

I nodded my head and smiled, but I was getting worried again, because I had seen a side of Shabazz that I had never ever known existed, and I just wondered, if things ever got thick on his end because of me, would he take me out as easily as he had Tut?

The same night that Tut had been killed, me and Shabazz went right back to fucking each other like rabbits. In fact, we never slowed down from our three- and four-a-day sex sessions. Shabazz never mentioned the killing, and I also never mentioned it. In fact, during the week that followed Tut's murder, the only time that I ever mentioned his name was when I told Shabazz that we had fucked up, in the sense that I should have at least gotten like ten grand from Tut's ass before Shabazz killed him. Shabazz agreed with me, but at that point what was done was done, and I had to make do the best I could and just figure something else out.

The following Thursday morning, about a week after Tut's murder, Shabazz and I were butt naked and asleep in Shabazz's king-size bed. I guess it was like almost six in the morning when Shabazz's intercom began to ring.

"Who the hell is that?" Shabazz asked in a groggy tone. He picked up his cordless phone that the intercom was wired to.

"Hello. Who?" Shabazz sighed. "Yeah, yeah, you can let her up." Shabazz hung up the phone.

"Who's that?" I asked as I sat up in his bed.

"Fuckin' Essence."

"Essence?" I asked with a lot of confusion in my voice.

"I don't know what the fuck this bitch want. I'ma just talk to her ass real quick so she can stop blowing up my phone."

"Don't let her know I'm here," I said as Shabazz got up and threw on some boxer shorts.

"I know that. Just chill here in the room while I talk to her."

Within seconds the doorbell was ringing, and Shabazz went to the door and opened it.

"What's the deal, baby? You got me all worried about you and shit, not returning my calls. What's up?" Essence spoke all loud like it was two in the afternoon, and not six in the damn morning with people still trying to sleep.

Shabazz said something in response to her, but I couldn't hear what he was saying as his words sounded muffled.

"I understand that, but you could've at least called me. I mean, you ain't come through and give me no dick or nothing, just disappeared on me."

My mouth fell to the floor when she said that because I had no idea that Shabazz had been fucking her.

After Essence said that, I heard the front door open, and then I didn't hear any more voices. I assumed that Shabazz must have walked her into the hallway so that I couldn't hear what the hell they were talking about. My instincts told me that something was up. I didn't like the way shit was looking. I knew that even if it meant me selling my ass on the street for money, then that would be what I would have to do. But I had to get out of Shabazz apartment, and on my own as soon as possible.

Five minutes later I heard the front door open and I just turned over and laid in the bed with the covers barely covering me and acted like I was sleeping. And the next thing I heard was someone go into the bathroom. I knew it was Essence simply because of the sound that her piss was making. It sounded like a woman squatting on the bowl and pissing and not forceful like a man standing over the toilet bowl and pissing.

"So you don't wanna introduce me to your lady friend?" Essence asked as she came out of the bathroom. She sounded as if she had walked into the bedroom, but I didn't want to turn my head in the direction of the bedroom door and look.

"Essence, I'll holla at you later," Shabazz replied. "I'm tired."

"So we good?" Essence asked.

"Yeah, I told you that already," Shabazz said, sounding annoyed.

"A'ight, babe," she said before exiting.

"What the fuck did she want?" I asked as soon as Shabazz stepped back into the room.

Shabazz scratched his head, and then he sucked his teeth and took off his boxer shorts.

"She ain't want nothing, she just wanted to know what was up with me and why I hadn't been to the club and she was asking me had I seen Tut."

I didn't respond. I just lay on my stomach and wondered, If Shabazz was fucking Essence, then what did she really know? Like when she had made that "lady friend" comment, I began to wonder if she was trying to mock me in some way.

You gotta get the hell outta here, Destiny, I said to myself just as Shabazz got in the bed and began rubbing on my ass. At that point I was definitely not in the mood for sex, so I moved his hand off of my ass.

Thankfully Shabazz didn't trip about it. He simply went on to tell me more of what Essence had said about how she was worried about Brazil's club and how she wanted him to help her get the club shut down.

"So you gonna help her with that or what?" In my mind I knew that Essence and Shabazz were in way too deep with each other for her to be asking him some shit like that, and it made me wonder just why he had really killed Tut.

Shabazz didn't answer me and instead he began rubbing on my pussy.

Not now! I thought.

Shabazz was persistent. I reached and felt his dick, which was harder than Chinese arithmetic, so I knew that he definitely wanted to fuck.

Just do it, Destiny, and get it over with.

Shabazz stroked his hard dick, and I opened my legs for him and let him do his thing. But the whole time that he fucked me, my mind was completely somewhere else.

Chapter Twenty-one

Brazil

Ihad just finished trying on this outfit that I was gonna wear to Magic City later that night when my cell phone started to ring. I had on a Christian Louboutin leopard-print pony hair shoes, a black Zac Posen Iconic jacket, and a tulip skirt and was admiring myself in the mirror.

"This shit is hot, right?" I asked Vegas, while retrieving my cell phone from my bag.

The call was coming from a blocked number, but since it was Thursday, Magic City's biggest night, I knew that it could be an important call. I decided to answer it. "Hello." I listened, as there was a pause on the other end of the phone.

"Brazil?" the caller asked.

"You called my phone, didn't you? Yes, this is Brazil," I answered sarcastically.

"Brazil, this is Destiny," I heard coming through my receiver, and I instantly recognized Destiny's voice. She had totally caught me off guard but not enough to make me catch an instant attitude. "What the fuck are you doing calling my phone?" I barked.

"Brazil, listen to me, first let me just say that I'm so sorry for everything that went down between me and you, I never got a chance to—"

"Sorry? You got the nerve to call my phone, and the first thing you say is you're sorry? Bitch, you fuckin' tried to kill me damn near right in front of my daughter, and all you can say is you're sorry?"

"Brazil—"

"Shut the fuck up while I'm talking," I screamed into the phone. "You let me spend the night at your crib like everything was all good, and then the next day you fuckin' tried to murder me? Destiny—"

"Brazil, just listen to me." Destiny screamed, cutting me off. "I know you know I'm on the run, and I know that I more than fucked up by crossing you the way I did. I know that. But right now I need your help, and at the same time I can help you."

"Destiny, I swear to God, just hang up this fuckin' phone right now because talking to me is only making shit worse," I replied.

"Listen to me, they plotting to legally shut down your new club," Destiny said.

"Destiny, you know what? FUCK you and FUCK whatever the hell you're talking about. And, I swear to God, you better hope you get caught and locked the fuck up before I see your ass!" I hung up the phone.

"That was Destiny?" Vegas asked me.

"Yeah, you believe she was calling my phone?"

"She desperate if she's calling you."

Vegas was probably right, but I could have cared less about how desperate Destiny was. What I did know was that she had probably gotten wind of how well Magic City was doing and was gonna either try to sweet-talk me into letting her get in on the action somehow, or she was gonna slick-talk me and set me up to finish off what she hadn't succeeded at when she shot me.

"She got balls the size of an elephant," Vegas said to me.

"Yeah, she do, but I tell you what, let her ass come by Magic City and I swear on Angie's life that the cops will be hauling her ass away in a body bag while they haul my ass off to jail. You better believe that shit." I was dead serious.

Chapter Twenty-two

Essence

My whole ride home from Shabazz's apartment, my mind raced back and forth about what I *knew* I had to do. The thing was, I just didn't know if I could violate my values and bring myself to do it, and that was rat out Shabazz.

I knew that if I didn't, that he was either gonna kill me or rat me out, so although snitching went against the codes that I lived by, there was no way that I could just sit around and not double-cross the person who was trying to double-cross me.

Shabazz had claimed that he didn't know what had happened to Tut, but I could see it in his eyes and I could just sense that he was lying. Shabazz had killed Tut. He would never ever admit that to me, but I was sure that he had killed Tut. I also knew that he was a cop, so he knew that if you properly get rid of a body after a murder that there basically is no murder if the authorities can't find a body. I could only imagine what he had done with Tut's body. And bringing things closer to home, I didn't want to be added to Shabazz's body count.

And even if Shabazz hadn't killed Tut, I reasoned that my relationship with him had clearly broken down and I knew way too much dirt about him. Dirt that could have his ass locked away for years. That also put me at risk of being killed by Shabazz.

But the thing that really had shocked the shit outta me and made me say that there was some kinda plot against my ass was that I had a strong-ass feeling that Shabazz had Destiny up in his crib. Although I wasn't certain of it, I knew that if Destiny was in Shabazz's crib and Shabazz never told me that she was hiding out with him, then there was nothing that I should trust about him.

When I had gone to use Shabazz's bathroom, his bedroom door was slightly ajar and I was able to see part of his bed. And what I saw was someone lying on their stomach underneath the bed sheets. The person's face wasn't visible, but one of their legs wasn't underneath the covers. It was exposed as it dangled from the bed. I could only see the person's calf and foot, but it was definitely a light-skin person and they had a tattoo with Chinese letters on their calf, which just so happened to be the same type of tattoo that Destiny had on one of her calves.

Essence, that was her, I said to myself. *Destiny is light-skin, she has a tattoo with Chinese letters on one of her calves, and she knows Shabazz.* I continued to think, trying to convince myself that it was Destiny.

But Destiny don't know that Shabazz is a cop, I thought to myself, as I crossed the Throgs Neck Bridge. *Essence, how the hell do you know what she knows about Shabazz? For all you know, Shabazz coulda been fuck-*

ing her longer than he was fucking you. And as far as I'm concerned, if I was on the run I would definitely feel safe hiding out with a crooked cop. I continued to talk and reason with myself.

By the time I made it into the driveway of my Bayside home my mind was made up on what I should do and just exactly who I should call.

Chapter Twenty-three

Destiny

Shabazz called in sick from work that Friday Essence had come by his crib. He also called in sick that Saturday and that Sunday. He wasn't actually sick. What it was, was that he just wanted to stay home so we could fuck.

In the beginning the sex with me and him was cool and everything was all good even if it was all the time. But it was way past extreme at this point, and I was getting tired of being his sexual outlet. The dude was hooked on porn, and for those three days that he had called in sick all we did was watch porno and sex each other nonstop.

Thank God, when Monday came he told me that he was planning on going to work but wasn't gonna go in until eleven o'clock.

I couldn't wait for him to leave. I had decided that I was gonna dip into a stash of money that he had locked away in a lockbox with one of his guns and take a gun and whatever money he had in there and then just bounce while he was away at work. I figured that he had to have at least five thousand dollars in that lockbox, because who would stash money in a lockbox unless it was a substantial amount?

But just after nine o'clock when I was in the shower, I heard a loud knocking sound followed by a thud and I also heard someone say something. I couldn't really make out what was going on, but the first thing that I thought was that Shabazz was knocking on the bathroom door and calling my name so that he could get in the shower with me. I quickly turned on the small FM radio that was hanging from his shower head so I could use that as an excuse as to why I didn't hear him calling me and unlock the bathroom door so that he could get in the shower.

As I adjusted the dial to Power 105's radio station I got scared as shit as it sounded like someone had just kicked the bathroom door off of its hinges. My heart started to beat fast from having been startled, and I pulled back the shower curtain just partially to see what the hell was going on. All I saw was a police officer dressed in a helmet and riot gear and holding a shotgun.

"NYPD!" the cop yelled as he grabbed the shower curtain with his free hand and yanked it to the floor, exposing my naked and soap-lathered body in the process.

I screamed and I pushed the officer's hand away as he tried to grab me. I threw a bar of soap at the officer and I hopped out of the shower and tried to run, but the cop pushed me and, with my feet being wet, I instantly fell to the floor.

"Stay on the ground!" the cop hollered at me with the water from the shower still running and the radio blaring in the background.

I tried to get up from off of the floor but I couldn't move. Before I could blink, the bathroom had filled up with cops. My face was to the ground, and my ass and elbows were facing the ceiling as the cops slapped handcuffs on me.

Gotdamn! I screamed to myself and cursed myself for not following my instincts and leaving Shabazz's apartment days ago when I first got a premonition that I needed to bounce for my own good.

"Do y'all know who my father is?" I could hear Shabazz angrily yelling from the other room. "Yo, if y'all don't take these handcuffs off of me right now, I swear to God, all of y'all asses is getting fired."

I could hear sounds being transmitted from an officer's radio. It sounded like a dispatcher trying to get confirmation that they had indeed apprehended my ass.

"That's correct, we have the suspect in custody," one of the officers who was in the living room replied into his walkie-talkie.

The cops then lifted me to my feet and read me my rights as they walked me outta the bathroom and into the living room, where I saw an absolute army of cops and police dogs and the whole nine yards. I could even hear a helicopter hovering outside of the apartment building.

"Can y'all at least let me put on some fuckin' clothes?" I yelled.

No one responded to me.

"Yo, I need some muthafuckin' clothes!" I yelled even louder. I was pissed off that I had been caught and I was even more pissed off that those white pig-ass cops were getting their cheap little thrills by looking at my naked black ass.

Finally one of the officers emerged from Shabazz's bedroom with a bed sheet and draped it over my body, while another officer held on to my cuffed wrists. As soon as the bed sheet was fully covering me up and the officer's hand that was holding my wrist was concealed, I couldn't believe he actually started rubbing on my ass.

Thhhh! I spit right into the officer's face. "Fuckin' pervert," I barked.

The cop yanked on my wrists and pulled them upward to purposely cause me pain. "Shut the fuck up. You talk when I tell your ass to talk," the cop screamed on me.

"Ahhhhhh," I yelled out in pain.

Shabazz looked like he was ready to explode. "Destiny, I jus' gotta make a call to my pops as soon as we get down to the precinct, and all of this bullshit will be over. We'll be a'ight, don't worry."

I blew air outta my lungs and I thought to myself, *Yeah, you might be a'ight 'cause you got that fucking badge.* But I knew that for me things looked bleaker than they had looked the first time I had been arrested.

Damn! I said to myself as I rolled my eyes and began to resign myself to my fate.

Chapter Twenty-four

Brazil

With everything that I had been through—being shot up, recovering from the shooting, and opening up Magic City, it hadn't left me much time for myself. Yeah, Vegas would help me out with Angie, but she was my responsibility ninety percent of the time. Needless to say, my sex life had been suffering big time.

Vegas and I would have sex every now and then, but that would just be based strictly on his baby-daddy privileges. Sex with Vegas had become boring and routine. So although I cared about him, I guess the fact that he wasn't my man was why there really was no passion when it came to sexing him.

But things were starting to look a lot better for me when I met this dude name LaTeek. LaTeek was younger than me. He was only twenty years old, but his sexy swagger made him come across as being more mature and older than he was.

I gave LaTeek my number the first night that I had met him. The next night he called me, and we ended up making plans to go out to eat that upcoming Sunday night at this upscale Chinese restaurant called Mr. Chow.

"**L**ook what the hell that bitch got on," LaTeek said to me as he made fun of a white girl who had walked into the restaurant. "That bitch ain't got no ass and she trying to rock them jeans like she a black girl."

I laughed and said to him, "LaTeek, you ain't right."

"Ah damn, that explains it, look at the nigga she wit'. His jeans is fuckin' tighter than hers!" LaTeek laughed and took a swig of the Bacardi and Coke he was drinking.

"Oh my God," I said in disbelief as I turned and looked. I couldn't believe it. I had never seen a guy with jeans so tight. "He gotta be a homo."

"That nigga ain't no homo. He got himself a white girl and you can't tell him that he ain't make it." LaTeek laughed.

The black guy with the tight jeans held his white girl by the hand and waited for the hostess to escort them to their table. And, wouldn't you know it, the hostess seated them right next to me and LaTeek.

It took everything that both me and LaTeek had to hold back from laughing at the dude and his tight-ass jeans. Eventually, though, we managed to block the guy out of our minds and we focused on each other and had a fun date.

LaTeek had the best sense of humor in the world, and I loved a guy who could make me laugh. He also had his own money. He had recently signed a half-a-million-dollar recording contract with Def Jam. And what impressed me the most was that LaTeek looked like a rapper, but he was actually an R&B singer who sounded a lot like the singer Jaheim.

When me and LaTeek left the restaurant we were thinking about going to a comedy club but we decided against it. We also thought about going to the movies but we decided against that too. Really it was me who was rejecting every suggestion that he was making simply because I was so turned on by him. I was horny as hell and hadn't had no good dick in a while, and I wanted to go back to my crib and fuck the shit outta him.

I was never the type to make a guy wait more than two weeks before letting him hit it, and at the same time I had also never let a guy hit it on the first date. But since I had gotten shot and gone through that near-death experience, it changed the way I looked at a lot of things, and I had made a vow to start doing me and living every day as if the next day wasn't promised.

So LaTeek and I made it back to my crib and we began watching P. Diddy's Bad Boys of Comedy on HBO on demand. And after about fifteen minutes or so me and La-Teek started kissing. I loved to kiss, especially when I was with a guy who knew how to kiss. LaTeek definitely knew how to kiss. After about a minute of kissing, my pussy was soaking wet and I wasted no time in making the first move. I stood up and unbuttoned my pants, quickly wiggled my ass out of it, and then sat back down on the couch next to LaTeek and we resumed kissing.

"Damn, that pussy looks good," LaTeek said to me while he kissed me. He started to kiss on my neck and then he moved his hand down to my soaking wet pussy and stuck his finger inside of me and I gasped with ecstasy 'cause the shit felt so damn good.

"Lay back." LaTeek slowly guided me until my back was on my living room couch.

I expected LaTeek to take off his clothes, but instead he went head first for my pussy and started eating me out.

"Wow," I softly whispered as his lips and tongue landed on my clit.

LaTeek began flicking his tongue back and forth on

my clit, sending uncontrollable chills up and down my body. Then he stuck one of his fingers into my pussy and slowly moved it around while still flicking his tongue on my clit. Other than the few women that I had been with in the past, no one had ever eaten me out so damn good and I was cumming all over the place.

Right after I came I was still breathing heavy and trying to catch my breath and LaTeek stood up, took off his pants, exposed his fat, hard, nine-inch dick, and quickly put on a condom.

I smiled and couldn't wait to feel his dick inside of me. And I got my wish because, before I could blink, he had me still on my back and both of my feet were on his shoulders as he fucked me hard and deep just like I liked it. Five minutes or so of LaTeek fucking me was all it took for me to start screaming and moaning uncontrollably, and I came for a second time.

Not much longer after I had came that second time, La-Teek began rapidly pumping his dick. I could tell that he was getting ready to cum and in seconds he did in fact cum.

"Gotdamn, that shit was good!" LaTeek yelled. He wiped some sweat that had formed on his forehead.

I sat up on the couch and I took LaTeek's condom off of his dick. I stretched the condom out and then I held the opening of the condom to my mouth and slowly let La-Teek's hot sperm roll into my mouth and I swallowed it.

"Oh shit, I ain't know you was wild like that."

"You brought that shit outta me."

The two of us then sat on the couch and I laid my head on LaTeek's lap. I was still horny. I was hoping that he was up for another round. So I got up and took off my top and bra and exposed my titties and walked off to my kitchen and asked LaTeek if he wanted something to drink. I brought him his drink, and after our ten-minute break, we were both going at it again for round two.

By the time round two was over, it was a little past midnight. I asked LaTeek if he wanted to spend the night. He said that he didn't mind, and after he and I had smoked some weed, we both fell asleep on the couch.

At like four thirty in the morning my eyes slightly opened and for a second I had forgotten where I was at because I wasn't in the familiar surroundings of my bedroom, and my daughter wasn't asleep next to me like she usually was. Angie wasn't home, and I was glad that she wasn't because, as soon as I closed my eyes again, my front door came bursting open.

"Police, put your hands in the air where I can see them," a cop shouted while shining a bright-ass flashlight in my eyes and blinding me.

"What the fuck?" LaTeek shouted as he sprang to his feet startled.

BANG!

"Ahhhh!" I yelled as I realized that one of the cops had just shot LaTeek.

"What the hell did you shoot him for?" I shouted at the cop. I immediately dropped to the floor to aid LaTeek. "Baby, you okay?" I asked.

One of the cops grabbed me and threw me to the ground and handcuffed me, while another cop held a shotgun to my head. Other cops ran to other parts of my house, ransacking the place.

I could hear one of the cops on his walkie-talkie telling someone that they needed a "bus" asap. And I could hear other officer shouting the word *clear* as they searched room to room and every nook and cranny of my house.

I didn't know why the cops were at my crib, and at that point my only concern was LaTeek's health. It looked like he had stopped breathing. "He's dying!" I screamed from my handcuffed position on the floor. "Call a fuckin' ambu-lance."

"An ambulance is on the way," one cop shouted at me.

Another cop read me my rights and placed me under ar-rest.

With my face right next to one of the used condoms that was on the floor, I closed my eyes and clenched my teeth. I was mad as hell and wondered just what the fuck was going on and why was I being arrested.

Chapter Twenty-five

Essence

Normally things would start winding down at like three in the morning at Promiscuous Girl and we would close the club at four AM. But in an effort to try and crush Magic City, I decided that Promiscuous Girl would keep rocking until six o'clock in the morning. And I also decided that I was gonna start promoting Sunday nights really hard so that Sunday nights at Promiscuous Girl would be just as live as Wednesday nights.

Being that a lot of people who had came out to Magic City to see Heather Hunter ended up being disappointed because the cops had shut the club down before she had arrived, I decided that I would capitalize on that. To promote our new six AM closing time I reached out to Heather Hunter's management and was able to get her for Sunday night.

I had my people contact all of the New York hip-hop radio stations so we could buy commercial time to promote the Heather Hunter event and the new closing time, but I made sure that the commercial stressed that Sunday night would be the night that she would be there and not Wednesday night.

The radio commercials had definitely gotten the word out, because by two AM that Sunday night going into Monday morning, Promiscuous Girl was beyond rammed from wall to wall. Heather Hunter arrived early. She performed one of her new rap songs and even agreed to get on stage and dance for all the fellas.

For like two hours straight, Heather Hunter got all the attention in the club, but the other dancers didn't hate on her because they knew that as soon as she finished her routine and took pictures and signed autographs they would get the spill-over effect and make more money than they would have made that night if she hadn't been there.

My whole Southside Jamaica, Queens crew that I had grown up with, they were in the club with me that night helping me to kick off the new closing time. I was dressed to kill in my Sergio Rossi patent-leather tie-up boots that I rocked with an Emilio Pucci classic signature embellished dress. I got compliments all night long, as I kept a drink in my hand and made my rounds throughout the club and mingled with everybody.

At a little past five in the morning an army of cops and detectives swarmed in on Promiscuous Girl. There were cops inside and outside of the club who had seemingly appeared out of nowhere. The cops didn't let anybody leave the club and they didn't let anybody else inside the club. And they ordered the lights be turned on and the music turned off. Then they ordered everyone to their knees and made everyone interlock their hands and place them behind their heads.

"Fuck all that shit!" I yelled as I calmly sat down at the bar. "Y'all muthafuckas better have a warrant." I purposely did not comply with their orders for me to get on the ground. I sipped on my drink like a diva. "I ain't doing shit until I see a warrant."

One of the detectives then showed me a copy of the warrant that was signed by a judge and asked me could I see it clearly.

"I'm reading it now. Just chill the fuck out for a minute." I wanted to appear like I had more control of the situation than the cops.

"A'ight, I read it. Now what?" I said to the detective.

"Rachel Wright?" he asked for confirmation.

"Yes, that's me."

The detective then told me that he had to place me under arrest.

"For what?" I asked with an attitude as I stood up.

The detective grabbed hold of my right wrist and placed it behind my back and then he grabbed my left wrist and placed that behind my back and placed the handcuffs on me.

In the background the crowd was unruly and verbally raucous and abusive to the cops, but they complied with the cops' demands and no one tried any slick shit.

"Can I at least finish my drink?" I asked the cop with a sinister smile while he read me my rights.

"Y'all know this is some bullshit, right?" I asked.

The detective didn't say anything else to me and he began to escort me out of the club.

"Hold up a minute," I said to the detective as I stopped dead in my tracks. "My office is right over there, that silver and gray door near the deejay booth. My bag is in there. I need that shit. I can't leave here without it," I said in all seriousness.

The detective smirked and then he nodded to his partner, who walked off toward my office. And less than a minute later the other detective emerged with my oversized Marc Jacobs bag.

"Is this the bag?" the detective asked me.

"That's the one," I replied.

One detective held on to my right forearm while the other detective held on to my left forearm, and they escorted me out of the club and into a waiting squad car that was in front of my club. Reporters and photographers feverishly snapped pictures of me and asked me questions as I turned my body and sat butt first into the back of the squad car.

I didn't respond to any of the questions that the reporters were asking me, but I made sure that I kept a confident smile on my face. And when I wasn't smiling, I tried my best to come across like the graceful diva that I was.

Chapter Twenty-six

Destiny

Two days after I had been arrested I found myself back on Rikers Island in the Rose M. Singer Center, better known as Rosie. I didn't have time to get down and depressed or any of that shit because word had gotten back to me that me and Shabazz weren't the only ones who had been arrested. Brazil and Essence had also both been arrested, and on top of that Brazil and Essence were in the same jail that I was in. So I had to be on point because I knew that as soon as I saw either Essence or Brazil that it was gonna be on fo' sho.

But as it turned out, I was wrong about the drama that I thought was gonna come my way when I saw Brazil or Essence. A week after I had returned to Rikers Island I got the shock of my life when Essence, who unbeknownst to me had managed to post her million-dollar bail, came to pay me a visit. She came walking into the visiting room with one of her homegirls from Southside, but based on the way she was dressed, I had a feeling that she wasn't on no rah-rah shit, but I still had to check her ass just to make sure.

"Essence, if you coming here on some bullshit, just let me know right the fuck now!" I said with a stone look on my face.

Essence was wearing a John Galliano petticoat, with a vintage Chanel cocktail dress and black leather strappy Giuseppe heels. She shook her head as she looked at me. "Nah, it's not even like that, Destiny." She sounded real subdued. "You remember my girl Carlita, right?" she asked, talking like everything was all good between me and her.

"Of course, I remember Carlita."

Carlita smiled and nodded her head a few times.

There was an awkward moment of silence and then Essence spoke up. "Destiny, you know we looking at serious football numbers on these RICO charges and conspiracy charges they hit us with, right?"

"Yo, I been sick over that shit ever since they locked my ass back up again. But, Essence, I'ma keep it real wit'chu, a lot of this shit is stemming from Shabazz and his ass being corrupt and all that. And, for real, you shoulda told me he was five-O 'cause—"

"Destiny, look, it is what it is. I shoulda did a lot of shit differently, but this is where we at right now. Me, you, and Brazil are all facing some serious shit and what I'm saying is we need to put all that other shit behind us and figure out how the fuck we gonna beat these muthafuckin' charges."

"Word is bond," Carlita added for extra emphasis.

Before I could speak, Essence said, "I'ma come see Brazil tomorrow and I'ma let her know that all of this bullshit between me, you, and her is all petty shit and we gotta get over all of it. And here's the thing, Destiny, my paper is on zero right now. Between the money I had to put up for this bail and the money that I gotta pay these lawyers, my ass is broke. But if you and Brazil can put all the bullshit behind y'all, you got my word, and she do too, that I'll sell the fuckin' club to get this money up for you and for Brazil to get y'all outta here and pay for your lawyers and all of that."

I looked at Essence to make sure that I was hearing her right.

"Destiny, I'm dead-ass."

I paused and looked at her, I was trying my hardest to figure her out.

"Why, Essence?"

"Destiny, at the end of the day, you and Brazil helped me build that club, and when you think about all the money we made, all the people we met, and all the fun we had, it all won't mean shit if we locked away for twenty-five years. And the bottom line is, if we fight this shit together, then we got the best shot at beating these charges. But if we stay on that petty bullshit, then we all gonna be doing them football numbers in prison. It's that simple. Just tell me how you wanna rock."

"How you gonna sell the club? Ain't all your shit frozen?" I asked.

"The club is in my mother's name. I can sell it. It's all good. All I need is for you to let me know what you wanna do." Essence looked at me, impatiently waiting for an answer.

I held out my hand and I waited for her to place her hand inside mine. "Thank you," I said as I touched her sweaty palms.

Essence told me that she had to leave and that she would be in touch with me through mail and bi-weekly visits. She also told me that she figured that she could get about three million dollars for selling the club but that it would probably take a minute to find a buyer for that type of real estate.

"It's all good," I said to her. "It's not like I got other options." I chuckled.

The truth of the matter was that I did have other options, and later that night as I lay in my bed I tried to figure out if I should seek out that other option, or if Essence was for real.

She bullshitting you, I said to myself as I stared into the room's darkness.

I decided that I would just wait to see how things played themselves out between Essence and Brazil before I made a final decision on my next move.

Chapter Twenty-seven

Brazil

"Essence, you're full of shit," I coldly said to Essence as she sat across from me all decked out in her high-end fashions.

"Brazil, I'm trying to help you out!" Essence replied with an attitude.

"Help me out?" I said, a twisted look on my face. "You wanna help me out? Why the fuck didn't you help me out when I was shot up and laying up in ICU? Essence, y'all fuckin' tried to kill me and you expect me to just overlook that shit? Not until I get locked the fuck up do I find out that Shabazz is a cop, but I'm getting hit with conspiracy charges and all of that shit, primarily because you was fuckin' wit' his ass! You fucked up, Essence. It was all about you, and that's why we in the situation that we in right now."

"Brazil, I know I fucked up, I know that shit, but like I told Destiny, and I'm telling you the same thing, if we don't come together on this shit, then all of our asses is gonna be doing like twenty-five years. Do you wanna be up in this bitch until your daughter is in her thirties? If you do, then just let me know, and I'm outta here right now and you can fight this shit on your own. But just listen to what I'm saying, Brazil. I'm telling you that I'm gonna get up the money to bail you outta here and I'ma put up the dough for the lawyers. Now if that don't prove that I'm sorry for fuckin' up, then I don't know what else to say. I'll admit to you, just like I admitted to Destiny, that it wasn't just me that built Promiscuous Girl. You and Destiny was right there wit' me every day grinding that shit out. So if I cash out and sell the building, it's not like I'm asking y'all to take a handout from me. I'm just giving y'all what y'all help build," Essence said to me in a real convincing matter.

I blew out air from my lungs and contemplated for a minute or so.

"Essence, this whole year has just been so fucked up for me. My ass is still in physical pain every day from getting shot. I'm getting all kinds of bullshit threats coming my way 'cause LaTeek died up in my crib. Vegas is constantly flip-flop on my ass, and then I always got my daughter I gotta deal with and take care of. This shit is a lot!"

"I know that, and that's why I'm here. You know me, Brazil. And you know that for me to come here, that I had to be on some real humble shit. You know that," Essence added.

Essence was right, I did know her and I had never known her to have a compassionate bone in her body. And I had also never known her to show any kind of humility at all. It was always all about her, and I couldn't see how all of a sudden to her it was now all about us.

The only thing that I could think was that Essence was scared as hell that either me or Destiny was gonna switch up sides on her and try and workout a plea deal to save our asses, and in the process it would mean the end to her *fabulosity.*

"Essence, I swear to God, the only reason that I'ma fuck wit'chu is because of my daughter. I wanna get the fuck up outta here and be with her—"

Essence cut me off. "Exactly, and we gonna make that shit happen. You got my word on that shit. And all I need is your word that we gonna completely put all that other petty bullshit behind us so that we can move on and beat these charges."

Essence held out her hand to me and then she looked in my eyes. I grabbed hold of her hand and I told her that she had my word.

Essence then stood up to leave with her friend Carlita. Before she left, she smiled and said to me, "Brazil, I gotta admit something, and Carlita is my witness that I been saying what I'm about to say."

"What?" I asked.

"You did the *damn thing* with Magic City!" Essence added.

She sounded genuine and sincere, and at that moment a huge smile splashed across my face because, as far as I was concerned, it was like Essence was finally admitting in her own way that I won and she had lost.

"No doubt." I nodded my head to her before watching her and Carlita walk off.

Brazil, if you wasn't locked up in this jail, you know that shit wouldn't have gone down like that between you and Essence, I said to myself as I made my way back to my cell.

Regardless of how well I had just acted in front of Essence, I knew that I was still holding a whole lot of anger and resentment toward both Essence and Destiny. And I knew that my biggest battle was now gonna be not letting that anger and resentment get the best of me.

Chapter Twenty-eight

Essence

That Friday morning after I'd made it back home to my crib from Shabazz's apartment in White Plains, the only thing that I could think was that I had to make my move before anyone else made theirs.

Without hesitation, the first thing that I did when I walked in my crib was call this dude named Sean Coleman. But, Sean, who I had met a few years back in Promiscuous Girl, wasn't just any regular dude. He was a black thirty-eight-year-old former attorney-turned-New York City-councilman who was running for mayor of New York City.

Sean used to come through to Promiscuous Girl before he began to gain notoriety as a politician. When he started to gain popularity I saw less and less of him at the club, but he made it a point to always check in with me every now and then. Although I know that Sean and his boys wanted to fuck me, I never did let him or any of his people hit it, but he was the hip, Sugar Daddy type, and him and his whole crew had ran through just about every chick who had danced in Promiscuous Girl.

Even though I never let Sean fuck me, he was always

respectful toward me. He always told me that if I ever needed anything from him that I had a green light to call him at any time. So here I was in late October 2006 and I was dialing his cell phone to take him up on that offer he'd made to me.

"Hello," Sean said with his deep-ass voice as he answered his phone.

"Sean, you ain't got my number programmed in your phone?" I asked.

"Who's this?"

"Oh my God, I am so offended! Sean, it's me, Essence," I said in a joking manner.

"Oh, wow! Essence, I'm sorry, babe. What's up? I ain't heard from you in a minute." Sean quickly switched up into his homeboy voice. "You still looking sexy?"

"No doubt, you know that," I said.

"Ain't this early for you to be calling me?"

"Yeah, actually I just came home from the club. I ain't even go to sleep yet, but I had to call you 'cause I got some heavy shit that I'm dealing wit' right now and I need your help wit' it."

"What's up? Talk to me."

"Well, some shit is about to go down with Promiscuous Girl, like I think me and my partners might get indicted on some serious shit. I know you used to be a lawyer and all that, so I wanted to ask you, if I decided to talk to the district attorney and, you know, cooperate with them and help them out, like how does that work?" I asked.

"Whoa! Okay, I wasn't expecting that, but here's the thing. The only time the district attorney and federal prosecutors work out plea deals and full immunity deals is when they feel like they'll get slam-dunk type of information that will just about guarantee them a conviction on the other side of the deal. You understand what I'm saying?"

"Yeah, yeah, definitely, and like I said, I got some real heavy shit that I wanna put out there to protect my ass because I know that my partners is about to snake me. You feel me?"

Before Sean could respond to me I continued talking.

"And, Sean, I thought about this, and what I got could even help you out?"

"What do you mean?" Sean asked.

"I'll be straight up wit'chu. We had all kinds of shit going on at Promiscuous Girl other than just liquor and lap dances. I'm talking about shit like prostitution and drugs and everything else that comes along with that. But the thing is we operated like we was God because we had the NYPD in our hip pocket," I explained.

"The NYPD?"

"Yeah, see, there's this cop named Shabazz and he served as a bouncer but he was our ears and eyes that would tip us off to different investigations and raids that would be coming our way, so we was always one step ahead of the law. And the reason I was saying this could probably help you out is because Shabazz's pops is like the number three man in the Police Department and with you running for mayor, you would be in charge of the Police Department and all of that. So imagine if you put it out there that there was all of this corruption on the current mayor's watch that *you* had to uncover? And then you sold it like, if you were the mayor, the people wouldn't have to worry about corruption like this." I waited for Sean's reaction.

Sean was quiet, and then he burst out into a chuckle. "Essence, you're serious about what you're telling me? I mean, you're being straight up, no chaser with me, right?"

"Sean, I'm dead-ass," I bluntly stated.

Sean burst out into a hearty laughter. "Essence, you do know that you just got my ass elected, right?"

The way things happened to play themselves out, my timing couldn't have been more perfect in that the election for mayor was about two weeks away, and from what Sean told me, the race was neck and neck between him and the current mayor, and that if he dropped a bombshell about police corruption that would definitely get him elected.

"Listen, I'm cancelling all of my plans for the day and we gotta meet right now," Sean said to me.

A huge smile came across my face because I knew that I'd made the right move. "Okay, so you want me to come to your office?"

"Yeah, you know where I'm at, right?"

"Definitely," I replied.

I was tired as hell but I knew that I had to make it to Sean's office so that I could draw first blood. And that was exactly what I managed to do by contacting Sean.

When I made it to Sean's office he and I talked for about a half an hour straight. He grilled me and took notes, repeatedly asking me some of the same questions over and over again, only he asked them in different ways. I knew that he was just trying to make sure that my story was straight and to see if there were any holes in it.

After Sean and I were done talking he placed a phone call to Gerald Shargel, who is one of the most prominent defense attorneys in New York. He had represented many famous clients, and most recently he had helped Murder Inc. CEO Irv Gotti and his brother beat a federal case that could have sent him away to prison for more than twenty years.

Sean had attorney Shargel on speaker phone and he introduced me and then he explained to Mr. Shargel exactly who I was, my background, and more importantly, what I wanted to do in terms of going forward to the district attorney. He asked Mr. Shargel if he would be interested in representing me.

Mr. Shargel systematically began to talk to me and ask me questions in order to feel me out. He was very receptive and seemed like he was highly knowledgeable.

"Essence, and Councilman Coleman, I'll shoot straight with you the way I do with everybody. The officer, Shabazz, he's the linchpin. And for the district attorney to even consider any kind of deal we would almost need a smoking gun. Essence, your testimony, no matter how credible it would be, it just wouldn't be enough to get them to move and that's because if this guy's father is high-ranking in the police department they could spin this thing ten ways to China and make things look dramatically favorable. I've seen it done on numerous occasions," the attorney explained.

"Mr. Shargel, when you say, 'a smoking gun,' do you mean like evidence against Shabazz that no one would be able to dispute?" I asked.

"Exactly," Mr. Shargel answered. "It's like the saying, go hard or go home. We either come to them with something so solid that they can't dispute it on any front, or we don't go to them at all."

"Well, I got that." I then went on to explain how I had the unregistered gun that Shabazz had attempted to use to threaten King Tut, and how I was sure that it had Shabazz's fingerprints all over it.

"Good, but not strong enough," Mr. Shargel answered.

"He's even housing Destiny, and she's on the run after escaping from Rikers," I added, thinking that would hold a lot more weight.

"Still, it's good, but even that's not strong enough," Mr. Shargel nonchalantly added.

"Mr. Shargel, I got the dude on tape taking money from me for a whole lot of underhanded shit. I got him on tape talking to me about a murder that he had pulled off. I got—"

Mr. Shargel cut me off and asked me to expound on what I had just said.

I went on to tell him how I always was worried about shit coming down on me and Shabazz being able to walk scot-free so, to guard against that, I would secretly video-tape shit and record conversations that he and I would have and save it, just in case I ever needed it.

Sean was grinning from ear to ear and was fidgeting with excitement in his chair.

I could hear the tone in Mr. Shargel's voice pick up and sound more confident as I explained just what I had on Shabazz.

So we ended the conversation with Mr. Shargel agreeing to meet with us later that day in his office, when I would bring in all of the evidence that I had against Shabazz, and from there we would plot how we would proceed.

And that is exactly what we did, and as it turned out, neither the feds nor the district attorney had any secret indictments against me, or Destiny, or Brazil, or anyone associated with us, but that didn't matter to me because I still felt in my heart that somebody was about to rat my ass out and I knew that I had to beat them to it.

I explained to Mr. Shargel that I wanted to protect my reputation from that of being a rat and I asked him if I went forward as planned, then how could I be protected from things getting out there with everyone knowing that I'd snitched. I also made it clear to him that I wasn't even remotely interested in no kind of witness protection plan either.

He explained to me that he couldn't guarantee what would or what wouldn't get out, but that if that was a reservation of mine, then he would try to get a deal where, although I had immunity or drastically reduced charges, the district attorney would arrest me and charge

me with the same or similar crimes as the other defendants, set a bail amount for me similar to that of the other
defendants, and then if the other defendants didn't take
guilty pleas, as we got closer to trial, which would be like
a year or so away, then and only then would it become apparent that I was actually cooperating.

"So what you're saying is that unless all of the defendants plead guilty, which is unlikely to happen, then we
can't ever really prevent it from getting out there that you
cooperated?" Sean asked Mr. Shargel for confirmation.
"The only thing we can do is delay when that information
gets out there."

Mr. Shargel nodded his head yes.

And with that, the stage was set for me to become a cooperating witness. Mr. Shargel contacted the Queen's
County District Attorney's office and told them what he
had and explained to them that I was willing to cooperate
with them.

The district attorney was very eager to meet with
Mr. Shargel, and when they met and he was able to lay out
all of the evidence that we had, they agreed in writing that
they would initially hit me with all serious charges and
then later drop those charges and only charge and prose-
cute me on a bullshit prostitution charge that I would
probably end up getting probation for.

I hated the prospects of being a snitch, but I have to
admit that I never ever knew that being a snitch could and
would feel so damn good. But it did feel good. It was like
I could sit back in the driver's seat and watch as most of
the moves that I had orchestrated were carried out.

Like I knew exactly when Shabazz and Brazil's cribs
were gonna be raided. And I knew exactly when my club
was gonna be raided and when I was gonna be arrested. I
knew how much my bail was gonna be set at, and I made
sure I had the cash on hand to post it. I knew that I would

stay in jail for a week and make it look like it took me a minute to get the money up. I knew exactly when Sean Coleman was gonna call his blockbuster press conference to get the word out about the "police corruption" and the pending indictments against me and my two lieutenants Brazil and Destiny, and my "den of prostitution and drugs" known as Promiscuous Girl strip club.

I was controlling politicians, cops, and district attorneys. I knew everything. And I loved every minute of it.

Who knew snitching could be such a powerful turn on? I would repeatedly laugh and say to myself as I waited for everything to fully unfold.

Chapter Twenty-nine

Destiny

Six months had passed since Essence initially told me that she would take care of my bail and my lawyers and all of that. For the most part during that time she kept in contact with me, always reassuring me that she was gonna make good on her promise as soon as the sale of the club went through. She explained that selling a three-million-dollar piece of property took some time and wouldn't happen overnight.

I completely understood that and I was patient. But what I didn't understand was how Essence would always be crying broke when she would speak to me, yet whenever she came to visit me she would be rocking a brand-new two-thousand-dollar outfit. The other thing that I couldn't understand was how she could find the money to pay for her lawyer, but as for her getting the funds for my lawyer, she would always claim to be "working on that." And when I would suggest that we all just use her lawyer, she would always adamantly refuse and say that would be dumb and would be no different than having one doctor deliver three babies by three different women at the exact same time.

Our trial was only five months away and I was still stuck with a fucking court-appointed lawyer who didn't know shit, other than to tell me that I should cop a plea and not even go to trial. It was so frustrating dealing with an incompetent lawyer, but I had no choice. As far as I was concerned, there was just no way that I was gonna take a plea. I just couldn't see myself going out like that. However, that all changed when I made one of my regular phone calls to Cathy.

"Destiny, didn't I tell you that Essence was gonna end up playing your ass?" Cathy said to me in her Puerto Rican accent.

"What happened?" I asked. My heart began to race.

"What happened is, she playing you."

"Cathy, what are you talking about?"

"She been telling you that she broke and ain't got no money and all of that, but she got enough money to open up a new club down in ATL."

"What?" I asked sounding both confused and in disbelief.

"Destiny, two different people told me about this new strip club down in Atlanta called Promiscuous Girl and they was telling me how some chick from New York came down there and opened it up and had shit popping off crazy. So I know a few people who moved down there from New York and I asked them to ask around and see if they knew anybody who knew about the club, and they all got back to me and confirmed that there's a new strip club down there called Promiscuous Girl," Cathy explained.

I was quiet on the phone and was breathing kind of heavy and just thinking to myself.

"Now if she ain't tell you about that shit, then she trying

to play you," Cathy reasoned. "And why would she be opening up a new club if y'all are supposed to be getting ready to go to trial?"

Cathy had asked the million-dollar question. When I got off the phone with her, I began to think that maybe Essence wanted to open the club before we went to trial, just in case we blew trial and got locked up she would have a form of income coming in. But that reasoning just didn't make much sense to me. So as I thought to myself for about an hour or so, it just hit me like a ton of bricks that Essence had to have plans of opening this club in Atlanta, and if she did, I knew that she had plans on being around to operate it.

That bitch been stringing y'all along all this time and now she getting ready to make a deal and rat y'all out, I thought to myself as my palms instantly got sweaty and my heart rate picked up.

I began to pace back and forth in my cell. And for the first time I couldn't wait to speak to my court-appointed attorney so I could tell him that I was ready to make a deal. *Fuck that bitch!* I thought to myself. I wasn't no rat, but if Essence thought that she was gonna rat me out and send my ass to jail, then she was sadly mistaken because I was gonna flip the script on her and make my move before she made hers.

Chapter Thirty

Brazil

A lot of the female corrections officers had stank atti-
tudes toward me because they were jealous of how
exotic and beautiful I looked. It was wild, because here I
was, locked up and shit, and still I had bitches with good
jobs and their freedom hating on me. But I knew that a lot
of the hate came as a result of the positive attention that I
would get from the male corrections officers. Many of
them knew me from my days as a stripper, so they were
always cordial and nice to me.

Everyone called the corrections officers by their last
names, and there was this one C.O., Officer Anderson,
who was cute as hell and was always coming on to me.
Around my third month in Rose M. Singer Center, Officer
Anderson approached me as I was heading back to my
cell.

"How's my favorite inmate?" he discreetly asked me
and then smiled with his perfect bright white teeth. He
looked a lot like the model Tyson Beckford.

"I'm a'ight," I replied with a smile. "And how's my favorite C.O.?"

"I'm good, but listen, how much for a lap dance?" Officer Anderson asked me and completely caught me off guard.

"Huh?" I said, a confused look on my face.

"I'm serious," he replied.

"Come on, Officer Anderson, stop playing," I said as I continued walking toward my cell.

"Yo, what about twenty dollars for a lap dance and a buck twenty for a VIP, if you wit' it?"

I thought to myself, *He can't be serious*, but I wanted to test him.

"A buck twenty? You like eighty dollars short," I replied, sounding seductive like I was in a strip club and trying to get money out of a baller.

"But you wit' that shit, though, for two hundred?"

I smiled and nodded my head and made my way back to my cell. I was sure that he was just bullshitting with me.

About a week later, Officer Anderson came up to me again and said, "Either today or tomorrow a money order for like two hundred is gonna arrive at the address that we have on record for you."

"What?" I asked.

"The two hundred for that VIP shit we spoke about," he replied.

I smiled and said, "Stop playing with me like that."

"Brazil, I'm dead-ass," he said. "Call your crib, confirm that shit. The next five nights I'll be working eleven at night until seven in the morning, so I'll come get you from your cell at like one o'clock in the morning, and we can slide off and make this happen," Officer Anderson explained. He sounded like it was a routine thing for him.

Sure enough, I called my crib, and my grandmother told me that a money order for two hundred dollars had come in an envelope addressed to me. I couldn't believe it, but I was happy as hell to get the money. I told my grand-mother to go to the post office and cash the money order, and to buy something for my daughter and for her to keep the rest of the money.

Later that night, Officer Anderson came to my cell and got me and he discreetly escorted me to this equipment room that had walkie-talkies and what looked like battery chargers for the walkie-talkies. The room was dark, and the only light was the hallway light that shined in through the upper half of the stained glass door.

As we made our way into the room I couldn't believe what I was about to do. I was nervous, but it was mainly because I was worried about getting caught. Officer Ander-son didn't say anything to me as we entered the room, and I didn't say anything to him.

He proceeded to unzip his pants and expose his dick. I went down on my knees and just began sucking on his dick. His dick got hard in no time, and from his reaction, I could tell that he was enjoying my head game. After his dick was rock-hard I began sucking on his balls and si-multaneously stroking his dick. Then I would put his dick in my mouth and suck on it, while stroking it with my hand. I kept alternating between his balls and his shaft and could tell that he was about to cum. I was getting really turned on.

"Hold on," he said, "I don't wanna cum yet." He reached down in his pants pocket and got a condom and then he instructed me to take off my clothes.

As I undressed, Officer Anderson put on the condom and as soon as I was fully undressed he had me sit my ass on a table that was in the room and he held my legs apart and slid his dick into my pussy and began fucking me missionary-style.

I hadn't had no dick in three months, so his shit felt good as hell, sliding in and out of my pussy. I was turned

on just from the fact that what we were doing was so
taboo, and I came in no time. I had to bite my hand to prevent myself from screaming and carrying on in ecstasy.

After a few minutes Officer Anderson came, and his
body collapsed on top of my body. He kissed on my neck
until he caught his breath.

"Oh shit," he said, whispering into my ear, "that shit
was better than I thought it was gonna be."

I smiled, and to boost his ego I said, "Yeah, that shit was
good to me too. You definitely know how to use that big-
ass dick."

Officer Anderson pulled his dick out of my pussy. He
took off the condom, and we both started getting dressed.

"So you do this all the time?" I asked.

"Nah," he quickly replied.

I didn't ask any more questions after that point and he
escorted me back to my cell. And when I made it back to
my cell and laid down to sleep for the night, it was like I
was on an emotional high as I thought about how I could
easily flip sexing the corrections officers into my new hustle that would at least allow me to get money to my
daughter and grandmother.

In the three months that followed that sexual tryst with
Officer Anderson, my hustle got to the point where I was
fucking a different C.O. at least two nights out of the
week. And in a span of ninety days I had made close to
five grand just from selling my pussy. It wasn't life-changing
money, but it was enough dough where I felt like I was in-
dependent and doing me, and didn't have to beg and bor-
row shit from people.

The other good thing that came along with fucking the
different C.O.'s was that they would help me out with a lot
of shit, like they would bring me in McDonald's and
Burger King and good shit to eat. They were able to put
Bacardi into the Coca-Cola drink that they would bring

me with my fast food, so I was able to get a good buzz going for myself a couple nights out of the week.

But they also helped me out with other shit that I couldn't do for myself. For example, one of the C.O.'s told me that his sister owned a Century 21 franchise and that he sold real estate on the side. So, knowing that, I had asked him if he could check on the value of the Promiscuous Girl club. I wanted to see if Essence was telling me the truth about it being worth three million dollars.

It took him a few days to get back to me, but when he got back to me with the information, he almost floored me with what he said. He told me that he had his sister check the public records at the courthouse and that she found out that the building was actually worth a little more than three million, more like three million seven hundred thousand, but that it was sold in December of 2006 for just under three million.

December 2006? I thought to myself.

If that was correct, then that meant that Essence had sold the building about two months after we had all gotten arrested. Yet she had been letting on to me for months that she was broke and couldn't wait to sell the building so that she could post my bail and get me up outta jail and get working on securing a prominent lawyer.

I instantly felt sick when I found out that information. And I felt even sicker when I realized that here I was selling my ass in jail for a couple hundred dollars and meanwhile Essence was out there living it up with a couple million in profit that she had made off the sale of the building.

I wanted to scream out in frustration, but I knew that I had to maintain. Essence was the best con artist around, but this was for damn sure gonna be the last time that her snake ass was gonna get over on me. Right then and there, I made up my mind that I was gonna somehow fig-

ure out a way to get up money for a halfway-decent
lawyer. And I only needed that lawyer to do one thing for
me and that was to represent me to help me work out a
deal that could reduce my charges in exchange for my testimony.

That was the only power and recourse that I had to get
back at Essence, and it was long overdue that her ass got
paid back for all of the underhanded shit that she had
pulled. If it meant that I would have to give my pussy
away for free to all of those C.O.'s, then that's what I was
willing to do, so long as I would be able to barter that into
them helping me to get a decent lawyer who could quickly
put things into motion for my ass.

Chapter Thirty-one

Essence

By April of 2007 the rapper 50 Cent had released a new hit single called "Straight to the Bank," and the hook went something to the effect, *I'm laughing straight to the bank with this huh huh huh huh huh huh ha.* Those words couldn't have been more appropriate for me. I had sold *my* club five months ago in December 2006 for $2,900,000, and considering that I only had a little over $700,000 left on the mortgage, it meant that I had made $2,200,000 in profit. So I was definitely laughing all the way to the bank. I'd also sold my house in New York and profited $300,000 from that sale so I was all caked-up and loving it.

My plan all along had been to sell the club and take the money and go down to Atlanta and buy a club down there, and that is exactly what I did. Only, I splurged my ass off and bought a convertible Bentley and $75,000 worth of jewelry.

The cost of living in Atlanta was so cheap compared to New York that I was able to buy a mini-mansion for me to live in for $600,000 and I also found a two-story warehouse in Buckhead that I purchased for $800,000. The warehouse was where I'd planned to open up the new Promiscuous Girl club.

I put $250,000 worth of renovations into my new club that I'd purchased in February 2007. By April the renovations were complete, and I began promoting for our grand opening.

I flew in six of my homegirls from Southside Jamaica, Queens so that they could live with me and help me get the club off the ground, and they had been living with me and helping me for the past six weeks. During those six weeks my homegirl Chanel came up with a brilliant idea for the new club. Since the club had two levels, she suggested that I fill the lower level with female strippers for the men, and the upper level with male exotic dancers for the women.

"Essence, the shit would be off the damn chain! Ain't nobody ever did that before," Chanel said.

Chanel was absolutely right on point with her prediction, and when we opened the club it was an instant smash hit from day one. The spot was so large that we literally had damn near one hundred female strippers and close to twenty-five male exotic dancers. And as far as regular customers, there had to be more than a thousand patrons up in the club and they were all there to spend money.

There was so much money flowing through that club, it was ridiculous. I had never seen anything like it. It was as if someone had walked through the club with garbage bags full of money and just dumped money throughout the club. The dancers had so much money that they were scooping it up with both of their hands and arms and running back to their lockers butt-ass naked and stuffing the money into their lockers and then heading right back to the dance floor to get more money.

We had these wind machines evenly dispersed through-out the club, which only created to the wild atmosphere in the club. The wind machines caused all the money on the floor to swirl around into the air, giving the appearance the money was raining from the ceiling.

So when you combined the butt naked dancers, the liquor, the boatloads of money, and the banging deejay, our opening night turned out to be something special. The upstairs with male exotic dancers wasn't as successful, but me and all of my homegirls could sense that it would just be a matter of time before we got it popping up there as well.

By the time we left the club it was about six o'clock in the morning, and I was feeling hungover from all of the liquor that I had drunk. My security and my homegirls were hungry, so we ended up going to Waffle House, where we ate until about seven thirty that Saturday morning.

One of my bodyguards asked me as I sipped on my orange juice, "How much you think we did?"

I smiled as I thought to myself, *What the fuck do you mean* we? But I didn't say that to him. "We did okay," I nonchalantly said.

I hadn't counted all of the money that we'd made, but I was sure it was well into six figures. When I was in New York I would always leave the club with about twenty thousand in cash, and the rest of the cash I would leave inside a safe that was inside the club. I had planned on doing the same with the club in Atlanta, but for no particular reason, I just felt like leaving the club that morning with all of the money that we had taken in.

After I paid the breakfast bill I reached into my bag and I counted out one thousand dollars and gave a thousand dollars apiece to each of my six girlfriends and to my three security guards.

"Gotta share the wealth," I said to my crew as I stepped into the front passenger seat of my Bentley.

As my bodyguard, whose name was Sincere, and who was also from New York, drove, I reclined in my seat and fell asleep. The food had helped me to feel a little bit better, but when we reached home, all I wanted to do was sleep. And that was exactly what I did. I headed straight to my room. I didn't even take a shower. I just took off all of my clothes, locked my bedroom door, and laid my ass across my king-size bed and was out like a light.

Around two o'clock that afternoon Chanel came knocking on my door like she had lost her mind.

"What!" I yelled in my groggy voice. I hated being woken up, especially if it was for some stupid shit.

"Did you order pizza?" she asked.

"Did I order what?" I shouted back.

"Some dude is at the door with like four pizza pies. You ain't order it?"

"Chanel, I'm fuckin' sleeping! I didn't order no pizza, but just pay for the shit and leave me alone. And turn that gotdamn music down," I screamed before closing my eyes and trying to go back to sleep.

I loved having my people around me, but with all of them living in my crib, ever since we'd got to Atlanta, it had been one big party. Twenty-four/seven there was weed smoking, liquor drinking, music blasting, and spades games being played. At times I just wanted nothing but peace and quiet and to be left the hell alone.

Two seconds after closing my eyes I got up and walked to the bathroom that was connected to my bedroom so that I could pee. And no sooner than I had sat my ass down on the toilet bowl, I heard all kinds of screaming and hollering and carrying on coming from downstairs. The first thing that I thought was that the guys were playing with the super soaker water guns and wetting the girls, but as I listened closer, I realized that real guns were being let off.

What the fuck is going on? I popped up off the toilet bowl and ran to my room and began squeezing my ass into a pair of jeans. But before I could get the jeans on I fell and ducked for cover as I heard the sound of rapid gunfire. It sounded like an Uzi or some high-powered shit like that.

I quickly turned on my closed-circuit security monitor that was on my nightstand. Looking at the monitor, I saw my front door swung wide open, and pizza boxes and pizza spilled onto my beautiful granite floors. Two dudes with guns were quickly moving throughout my living room and first floor of my two-story house, and I saw two of my homegirls on the floor, and they weren't moving.

Muthafucka! I said to myself. I grabbed my small .20 handgun from inside my purse.

"Essence, open the door! Hurry up," Sincere frantically pleaded with me after tapping on my door.

My heart pounding, I ran to my door and opened it. "What the hell is going on?" I asked. I was happy as a muthafucka to see Sincere.

"I don't know. Niggas just came through the front door blasting." Sincere grabbed me by the wrist and led me toward my bathroom. My jeans were around my ankles, as I still hadn't had a chance to fully put them on. I knew things were serious, because Sincere didn't even do a double take when he saw my naked-ass pussy.

"Just go in the bathroom and get down on the floor and stay there," he said, pushing me in the bathroom and closing the bathroom door behind me.

I finally managed to get my pants pulled up. As soon as I did that, I heard more gunshots, which sounded like they were right outside my bathroom door. With the shots being so close to me, my instincts told me that if I stayed inside that bathroom I wouldn't make it out alive. So, without hesitation, I opened the window that was above my toilet bowl and I stepped on the toilet bowl, turned my ass toward the window and I slowly guided my body out of the window feet first until my hands were the only thing gripping the window seal.

My feet dangling about twenty-five feet above the ground, I was leery about jumping, but as soon as I heard my bathroom door get kicked open, I loosened my grip on the window seal and dropped to my concrete patio below. Pain instantly shot through my body as I came crashing to the concrete. My face hit my knees, and I felt like I had chopped off my tongue with my teeth.

I agonized in pain for all of about five seconds. I turned and looked toward the window that I had just come out of and saw a gun being pointed at my ass. Adrenaline or something jolted through my body, and I bolted and ran as fast as I could toward my neighbor's house as shots ricocheted off the ground all around me. As I ran with my bare feet scraping the ground and my titties bouncing in the air, I was certain that I was gonna die.

"Die, you fuckin' bitch!" the gunman yelled while continuing to squeeze the trigger.

I was hyperventilating as I ran, just hoping that I could make it to safety. Just as I reached my neighbor's back porch, I tripped and fell to the ground. I scraped up my hands and knees in the process, but I quickly got up and started frantically banging on my neighbor's door with my bloody hands.

"Katrina! Katrina! Open the door. Hurry up! Open the door!" I desperately pleaded.

I didn't even know if my neighbor was home, but if she wasn't, then whoever it was that was trying to murder me was more than likely gonna accomplish their mission.

Chapter Thirty-two

Destiny

"**D**estiny, they're offering to reduce the attempted murder charge down to manslaughter, they're gonna reduce the conspiracy charge, and the RICO goes out the window," my lawyer explained to me as I sat across from him pissed the fuck off.

"But you don't understand. If I take that, then I'm still looking at fifteen years," I pleaded in a desperate voice to my lawyer.

"And if you take your chances at trial, then you're looking at twenty-five to life. Take the deal and you'll be out in ten years," he added, as if ten years was a piece of cake.

"I don't know." I shook my head as I weighed my options.

My plans of snitching to get myself off to make it better on myself didn't go as I had planned. And I must say that I had to give it up to that bitch Essence. Apparently she had beat me to the punch in securing her deal with the district attorney and was getting ready to take all our asses down. So the district attorney had no real incentive to work with me. And with the way things were looking for me, it seemed like copping out to the fifteen years was gonna be my only option.

If we were playing chess, Essence would have definitely been getting ready to checkmate my ass. And to put more salt on my wounds, I kept hearing from my people down in Atlanta how they felt like Essence was getting ready to blow with the club down there.

The only power that I had to get back at her ass was to sic some of my goons on her and kill her ass. If I had to do time in the clink because of her, then there was no way in the world I was gonna sit around and let her ass continue to breathe.

I had reached out to these two thug niggas from Roosevelt, Long Island to help me out with my plans to get at Essence. They were stick-up kids by nature, so sending them down to ATL was nothing, just as long as I told them that there would be a payoff for them in the end.

I broke down to them how Essence always left the strip club with like twenty thousand dollars and better on a big night and no less than seven grand on a slow night.

As we sat and hatched the plan, one of the goons, named B-2, asked me, "So what's in it for you?"

"I'm looking at fifteen years on account of this bitch, so y'all niggas would be doing me a favor. You feel me?" I said with a devilish smile.

"No doubt, no doubt," B-2 replied. "But, Destiny, you sure this bitch is holding, right?"

"B-2, I know she sitting on a couple million right now. Where she holding it, I don't know, but you got my fuckin' word that when that club opens up she's gonna have that shit crackin' up in there and she leaving there wit' twenty G's and better! I wouldn't send y'all down there for no bullshit," I added with emphasis, all the while trying to keep my voice down.

"A'ight, so we on it," B-2 said. "Me and Bimmy gonna go

down there and handle this shit. You know when she opening the club?"

I shook my head and replied, "Nah, I'm just getting my info in bits and pieces up in here, you know what I mean? I don't even got the address to the club or none of that. All I know is that it's up in Buckhead."

"I got people down there. It's all good," Bimmy added.

The two of them soon departed. I knew their stats and how thorough they were, so when they said they was gonna handle something, then it definitely would get handled.

But what was so wild was that when Bimmy and B-2 had made it down to Atlanta they didn't even have to handle that situation for me because apparently someone had beaten them to the punch, in terms of trying to snuff the life outta Essence and her whole crew.

As it turned out, Bimmy and B-2 basically had wasted their time traveling all the way to Atlanta for nothing and were pissed the fuck off at me, and were thinking that I had been trying to play them. In reality, though, that couldn't have been further from the truth, and I reasoned and explained to them that what had happened was that Essence had more than likely had a string of muthafuckas who wanted to see her dead and who were gunning for her and who'd just acted quicker than we had.

Eventually I was able to calm down Bimmy and B-2, and as soon as that issue had subsided, I had another pressing issue in New York that I personally wanted to handle. And she went by the name of Brazil. Yeah, if I was gonna cop out, then I had to bring it to her ass.

There was a cool-ass corrections officer supervisor named Angela Dickinson who was about ten years older than me. She was from Queens like I was, and we knew a lot of the same people. So I had some of my people talk to C.O. Dickinson for me, and I got them to convince her to work it out where she'd "mistakenly" have me and Brazil cross each other's path in the mess hall. All I needed was five minutes with Brazil so I could wear that ass out.

And as I sat about twenty yards away from her looking real incognito, that was just what I planned on doing. I hadn't told anybody what I was planning on doing because I didn't want anybody to tip her off.

Brazil was sitting down bullshitting with some other bitches, and none of them paid me any mind as I walked toward them.

"What's up, Brazil?" I said as I stopped and stood still behind her.

Brazil turned to look to see who was talking to her, and I reached back and punched that bitch flush in her face.

Baow!

I felt like I had broken Brazil's nose. I could hear her grimace in pain, but her pain didn't stop me from landing three more flush blows to her grill. Then I grabbed her by her shoulders and yanked her ass to the ground and started stomping on her ass.

"I should kill your stupid ass," I said as I continued to wear that ass out.

Brazil was trying to get to her feet and swing on me at the same time, but she accidentally slipped on some food that was on the floor and her ass fell hard to the ground. I continued to waylay her ass.

"Break this shit up," the corrections officers yelled as they rushed in to break up the fight.

I had a fistful of Brazil's hair and wasn't letting go as the C.O.'s tried everything they could to pull us apart.

"Let her hair go," they ordered me.

"Fuck this snitch-ass bitch." I spat in Brazil's bloody face.

One of the C.O.'s yanked my arm and freed Brazil from my grip, but I still had a handful of her hair in my hand.

I opened up my hand and let Brazil's hair fall to the ground. And she and I both looked at her hair as the crowd of inmates egged us on in the background.

I hollered at Brazil, "It don't matter how long I'm locked away for 'cause I'ma stay in that ass! You hear me, bitch?"

Brazil looked stunned, dazed, woozy, and embarrassed. She didn't say anything in response. All she did was twist her lips and look pitiful, as the C.O.'s carted me away and probably took her ass to the infirmary to get patched up.

Chapter Thirty-three

Brazil

The day that Destiny snuffed me in the mess hall just happened to be the same day that my daughter Angie and my mom were coming to see me. Unfortunately I ended up not seeing them because I had spent the majority of my afternoon in the infirmary getting my eye attended to.

Destiny had caught me with some good flush shots to my face and in the process left me with my right eye swollen shut and the rest of my face looking like I had been on the losing end of a twelve-round championship prize fight. I cherished every moment that I got to see my daughter, but with the way my face was looking, I was actually glad that Angie, and my mother for that matter, hadn't seen me all bruised up and shit.

What was weird though was that it seemed like Destiny had knocked some sense into my head when she suckerpunched me. For some reason that night while I laid in my bed I realized that enough was enough and that I had to be the bigger person in terms of stopping the back-and-forth catfighting and backstabbing nonsense that was going on. I was in jail, for crying out loud, and I was still going through the same shit that I had been going through when I was out on the street.

To me all of the drama between Destiny, Essence, and myself came down to each of us trying to prove that we were more powerful than the other. And that night as I lay in my bed, something that my grandmother would constantly say to me just sort of clicked in my head. And for some strange reason I finally understood what she meant when she would always say, "Baby, you have to learn to be meek like Jesus was, and as soon as you embrace that, you'll be fine."

I would always tune out whenever my grandmother started with the Jesus talk because, for one, I never understood what the hell she was talking about, and number two, I was just not that interested in that whole religious thing.

At the end of her "Jesus speech," my grandmother would always add, "You see, baby, to be meek simply means to have a whole lot of power, and to have that power under control."

As I lay in my bed I could hear my grandmother talking to me like she was right next to me. I could hear her voice explaining to me how powerful Jesus was, yet He would never use His power to seek revenge.

"That's how you gotta be, baby," the voice in my head said.

Right then and there, I decided that the bullshit was gonna stop on my end. I was gonna reach out to my court-appointed lawyer the next day and tell him to forget about trying to convince the district attorney to work out a deal for me in exchange for my cooperation. The DA wasn't really being that receptive to the idea to begin with, so there was no sense in me trying to exert control over a situation that I had no control over. And it made absolutely no sense for me to keep selling my ass to the C.O.'s just so I could try and come up with the money for a new lawyer.

I also decided that I was gonna overlook the blows that I received from Destiny. I made up my mind that I wasn't gonna concern myself with Essence and the fact that she was living it up at my expense. What I was gonna do was stay focused on doing me and also stay positive in my thinking about the trial, which was quickly approaching. I knew that I had the power to do those two things, and if I exercised that power over those two things and only those two things, I figured that I would be a'ight.

Chapter Thirty-four

Essence

Thank God for me that my neighbor Katrina was home. She'd heard me banging on her door with my frantic pleas, and ushered me into her home and to my safety.

"Oh my God! Essence, what's going on?" Katrina asked me.

"I don't know. They just ran up in my house and started shooting. I was 'sleep and—"

Katrina cut me off. She began speaking to a 9-1-1 operator, telling them that she needed an ambulance and the police asap.

"Katrina, look out the window and see if you see anybody," I nervously told her, fearing that the shooters were still coming after me.

Katrina ran to her living room window and peeked outside. She claimed that she only saw other neighbors milling about outside my house.

"Essence, lay down on the floor and raise your leg up," Katrina ordered me. "Wow! This doesn't look good at all. Look at all this blood!"

I followed Katrina's instructions. I didn't realize that my

leg was bleeding as bad as it was. I had felt the stinging sensation while I was running from my patio, like I had gotten hit with a leather belt or something, and I just figured that I had cut it or hurt it when I jumped from the window. But with so much blood flowing from my leg and spilling and splattering all over Katrina's floor, I realized that I had to have been shot.

Katrina ran to another room and came back with two huge beach towels. She told me to cover up my chest with one of the towels, while she wrapped the other towel around my upper thigh.

I screamed out in pain as Katrina tied the towel into such a tight knot.

"I gotta put pressure on it to stop all of this blood," she explained.

I nodded my head and told her that I understood. Right at that point Katrina's doorbell began ringing. I knew that it had to either be the neighbors or the paramedics, because killers wouldn't take the time out to ring the bell.

"She's over here," Katrina said to the police officers and paramedics.

The cops and the paramedics both began asking me questions at the same time and I couldn't decipher what was going on.

"Hold still, Miss. We're gonna have to cut your jeans in order to get a better look at that wound," the black female paramedic said to me.

I nodded my head and winced in pain.

"Miss, do you live next door?" one of the cops asked me.

"Yes," I replied.

"Can you tell me what happened?"

"I was asleep upstairs in my bedroom, and the next thing I know is my people woke me up and I heard gunshots and jumped out my bedroom window."

"Did you see who was shooting?"

"Nah," I answered.

The cop asked me some more questions, but I tuned him out as I heard the paramedics talking to each other and saying that it looked like one of my major arteries had been punctured.

"What does that mean?" I asked.

The paramedics looked at each other and told me to just relax and that everything would be okay.

The next thing I knew, I was being hoisted onto a stretcher and brought outside to a waiting ambulance, and when I got outside I looked and saw about four cop cars and two ambulances. The cops had roped off my house and my neighbor's with yellow crime scene tape.

Immediately an alarm went off in my head as I realized that I didn't see any of my people outside. I didn't see Chanel, Sincere, nobody.

"Miss, hold up a minute," I said to the paramedic that was pushing my stretcher. I tried to sit upright.

The paramedic, who by that point had learned what my name was, instructed me, "Essence, you're gonna have to lay down."

"Nah, I gotta go inside my house." I hopped off the stretcher and, with one of my pant legs cut and swinging in the air and all kinds of gauze wrapped around my leg, began limping toward my front lawn.

The cops grabbed me and told me that there was an active crime scene and that I wouldn't be allowed back into the house until their investigation was over.

"A'ight, okay, I'm coming," I said to the aggressive paramedic who was grabbing on to my shoulder and trying to pull me toward the ambulance.

"Can you just tell me if my people are okay inside the house?" I asked the cop with wide eyes, my nerves on edge.

The cop looked at me. I know he wasn't allowed to say anything to me, but his expressionless look said it all.

"Everybody?" I asked, hoping the cop would either not answer me or lie to me.

The cop barely nodded his head one time, but it was enough to make me lose it. It was like all of my energy was instantly sapped out of me.

"Oh shit, no! Nooooh!" I hollered and collapsed to the ground.

The paramedics quickly got me back to my feet and onto the stretcher and into the waiting ambulance and whisked me away to the hospital, where I had to have emergency surgery to repair my punctured artery which, according to the doctors, nearly took my life.

As it turned out, I survived the shooting, but after the surgery I learned something shocking that made me wish that I had been killed along with all of the rest of my friends who had been murdered in my home. Yeah, the detectives came by and showed me multiple crime scene photos that depicted all of my friends dead, bullethole-riddled bodies sprawled throughout my house. And while the photos were gruesome, it wasn't as shocking as what I had found out.

There were other photos that the detectives showed me where the letters NYPD were spray-painted onto two of the walls in my house. And while that immediately made me believe that Shabazz had gotten some of his police people to try and silence me, that too wasn't as shocking as what I had just learned.

See, I had lost mad blood, and the doctors had to give me a blood transfusion in order to replace all of the blood that I had lost. Prior to giving me the blood transfusion, they had to run tests to determine my blood type and shit like that. After they'd run the different tests that they had to run, they told me that one of the tests had came back positive for the virus that causes AIDS.

When I realized that the doctors weren't bullshitting me

and were serious about me having HIV, my entire body went numb. Aside from me feeling like I was about to puke my brains out, I didn't feel anything and I didn't care about anything.

At that point I could have cared less about the hundred grand that the shooters had taken from my home after murdering all of my friends. I didn't care about my Bentley. I didn't care about the club that I owned or the money that I had in the bank. Nah, I didn't care about none of that material bullshit 'cause the truth was, I would have given up all of that material shit in a heartbeat in exchange for a clean bill of health.

Matter of fact, I would have even traded places behind bars with Destiny and Brazil in exchange for the doctors to not have told me what they told me. But the reality was, the doctors had confirmed my HIV status.

In fact, over the course of the next two days the doctors and lab techs ran all kinds of tests on the blood banks that had supplied me with my blood for the transfusion, and none of it was tainted. They'd also swabbed blood from the clothes I was wearing on the day that I'd been shot, and tests confirmed that I had been HIV-positive before I'd been shot. Yup, that was my sad reality.

As I lay in my hospital bed recovering from my wounds, the only image that constantly replayed in my mind was the image of me catching King Tut fucking that nigga Joystick in his ass. Although I'd lived a promiscuous lifestyle and had had my fair share of sex partners, I was convinced that King Tut and his homo-thug ass was the one who had infected me. I had never seen this shit coming, and I didn't know what the fuck to do about it or how to handle it.

Chapter Thirty-five

Destiny

By the summer of 2007 I was shipped off to an upstate prison in Fishkill, New York, where I began serving my fifteen-year prison term. Considering that I had just turned twenty-four, it meant that the prime years of my life would be spent behind prison walls and I wouldn't be seeing the light of day until my thirties.

Instead of just serving time, I planned on letting my time serve me, so my first day at Fishkill I started writing a book that I planned to have published. I had always loved reading street novels and erotic novels, and I knew that I had the talent to write a book myself. Plus, from all of the people that I knew, I had a crazy connection with one of the editors at one of the major publishing houses in New York City, so I knew that if I did my part and penned a hot book, I would be able to get a six-figure contract. And I knew that it would be hot, because all I had to do was write about what I knew, which was sex, money, and murder. I had lived that life, so I was more than qualified to write about it.

I had planned on calling my book *Promiscuous Girl* because it was a hot title and also because I knew that it would get under the skin of Essence and Brazil to see me making money off a book with that title. Getting under the skin of Brazil and Essence was also going to become a full-time vocation of mine. I realized by copping out and deciding to go to prison, in some respects, meant that I was surrendering and waving the white flag. And physically that's what I might have been doing and physically I had probably lost the war with Brazil and Essence, but I knew that wars were also fought psychologically. And so I planned on psychologically torturing both Essence and Brazil from behind prison walls. I figured that as long as I could get in their heads and get under their skin, then I would continue to yield power over them.

After taking a break from working on my book, I took a pen and paper and began writing a letter to Essence. I wasn't sure where she lived, but I did have a flyer for her club down in Atlanta, where I sent the letter.

Essence,

What's up, ma? By now I'm sure that you heard that I copped out, and if you didn't know that I already started serving my time, then I'm sure you can see the return address on this envelope. So you know where I'm writing you from.

There's a big difference between me and you, Essence. My destiny may have been to come to prison, but I'd rather have that as my destiny than to have the essence of my character be questioned. And I chose my destiny, whereas the essence of who you are can't change because that's who you are by nature. You always been a fake-ass bitch and I always been a real-ass bitch, and that's why I copped out and decided to come upstate and do my time like a true soldier. You, on the other hand, decided to rat motherfuckers out in order to save your own ass. And you know why you did that shit? You did it because that's the essence of who you are. You a fucking snitch-ass bitch and you gets no more respect in the hood. And just like the true bitch that you are, you ran off to Atlanta so that you wouldn't have to be in your own hood 'cause you know that you can't get respect in the hood no more. It don't matter how much dough you got, you can't buy respect.

You tried to buy respect by bringing your crew with you to Atlanta and look what happened. I bet every night when you go to sleep you see Chanel and Sincere and the rest of your crew that you caused to lose their lives. Yeah, you tried to take them down to Atlanta to insulate yourself from the reality of who you are and now look. You ended up ruining the lives of good people and that's because you ain't nothing but a fuck-up, and anything and everything that you do, in the end, it's gonna flop and fail because the person behind it ain't real.

I knew from day one that you wasn't real, and that's why I had no problem fucking Tut or fucking Shabazz. You thought that I didn't know how you was getting down with Shabazz? That's laughable. But there's a whole lot of shit that I know that you don't think I know. The real question though is, did you know the shit that I know? I hope so, because it's always the shit we don't know that ends up killing our ass. It's crazy, right?

Holla back at ya girl!
Crystal Jackson
a.k.a.
Destiny

I ended my letter like that because I purposely wanted Essence to feel like I had always been one up on her ass. Even though I hadn't known for how long Shabazz had been fucking Essence, she didn't know what I knew, so I knew that by putting it out there that I did know about her and Shabazz, it would make her think that I had been out-foxing her all along.

See, I had never ever let anyone know that I was sick. Literally I was sick in the sense that I had been walking around with "the monster" ever since I was eighteen years old. It was my promiscuity at such a young age that caused me to get the disease, and once I learned that I had HIV, I looked at it as a death sentence. And if I had to die, then so did all of those foul-ass niggas who looked at me as nothing but a good light-skin piece of ass. At least that's how I reasoned it in my brain. And, besides, if a nigga was dumb enough to run up in me raw, regardless of how good I looked, then he really had a death wish that I had nothing to do with.

It was all good though, because although I had really liked Tut, the largest part of my motivation in fucking with him was so that I could really get at Essence, and even though I was behind bars I was certain that I had ac-complished my goal.

I wasted no time, and right after writing that letter to her I started writing one to Brazil.

Brazil,

What's good with you? I wanted to reach out to you and let you know that it brought tears to my eyes when I found out that you was actually a real down-ass chick. You got some big balls to take your case to trial. Actually it's a beautiful thing and it shows who you really are. I was thinking about that shit last night and I really felt bad because I was like, you ain't really a bad person and therefore it wasn't right for me to fuck your baby's father the way I did. Especially the way I was hollering and carrying on, and your daughter was right in the other room. That was mad disrespectful, and if it means anything, then I apologize.

But I'm sure you can relate to how it is when you ain't have no dick in a while and you end up just doing whatever it is that you have to do to get some. That's all it was between me and Vegas. It was just a one-time thing— but then that one-time thing turned into two times, and that turned into four times, and by the time we ended our little fling, I would say I only fucked him about ten times in total. But I'm sure you know how it is. I mean, you know, with the way you been breaking off a piece of your ass for all the corrections officers. You feel me?

Give Vegas my address and tell him to holla at me. Kiss Angie for me when you see her.

A'ight, I'm out. I'll holla.

> *Crystal Jackson*
> *a.k.a.*
> *Destiny*

P.S. I got a whole lotta other shit that I think you should know about. Shit that I was always too scared and insecure to share with people. But it's something that I think you need to know. Actually Vegas DEFINITELY needs to know, because it's always the shit we don't know that ends up killing our ass. It's crazy, right?

I felt so good when I was done writing those letters. And I knew that I was going to make a habit out of it and it would be a tough habit to break. I needed those letters to serve as a form of therapy because, the truth of the matter was, I had no idea how I wasn't gonna go insane sitting up in that prison with HIV.

Ever since I had found out that I had HIV I'd become hurt and bitter and I used sex, my sex appeal, and my flashy status to help medicate the pain and the bitterness that I had buried for the six years that I'd walked around HIV-positive. But now the sex, my sex appeal, and my flashy lifestyle were no longer at my disposal, and neither were the people who I loved and felt that I could trust.

The people who I thought were in my corner, they turned out to be fair-weather friends. Two months into my prison stay was all it took for me to start seeing who my real friends were. Most of my people stopped taking my phone calls, and all of the people who I did make contact with, they all had excuses for why they couldn't take the long seven-hour trip to come visit me in person.

When I was the hottest stripper in New York everybody loved me and wanted to be around me, when I had money from running the hottest strip club in New York everybody loved me and wanted to be around me, but now that I was locked away and out of sight I was out of mind.

The only thing that proved to me was that people are fake and phony and were only around me so that they could use me. Therefore if my destiny was to end up in prison with HIV, it was all good because I knew that by being the promiscuous girl that I had always been, in the end I would hurt far more people than the number of people who had hurt me.

I was determined to win even when I was defeated. It was my Destiny.

Chapter Thirty-six

Brazil

My trial started on Monday September 3rd, 2007 inside of the Queens Criminal Courthouse. The courtroom was packed with a bunch of my family members and supporters, and also a lot of media. I was nervous as hell because just that past Friday, in a separate trial, Shabazz had been convicted on first-degree conspiracy, and everyone was saying that he would have gotten off, had Essence not testified so convincingly on the prosecution's behalf.

Essence was absent from the courtroom on the first day of the trial during opening arguments and on the second day of the trial. That was because the prosecution had called a lot of insignificant witnesses. It was like they were trying to create this big buildup of drama that led up to Essence's testimony. And by the third day of the trial the drama had reached its peak when she showed up in the courtroom dressed like a high-ranking banking executive and nothing like the wild strip club owner that she really was.

Essence sat in the front row of the courtroom and was flanked by two beefy Italian dudes in Armani suits. She had cut her hair into a short-cropped style, and her hair looked very shiny and sleek. I had never seen her with that particular style, but it fit the shape of her face. I had to admit, she looked stunning as she rocked the new hairstyle and a pair of shades that looked like they cost fifteen hundred dollars.

Essence, with her signature MAC makeup and lipstick, was wearing a black Ann Taylor flounce skirt, a black two-button mid-jacket with a blue silk-river shirt, and a small Gucci handbag rested in her lap as she sat with her legs crossed.

I couldn't help but slightly turn my body and stare at her as she donned her poker face and looked straight ahead. She looked very serious and determined and kept that look until she was called to take the witness stand to be sworn in.

She stood up in her high-heel shoes, slowly removed her shades and folded them and put them in her bag, and confidently walked toward the witness stand like she owned the courtroom, leaving a trail of her Britney Spears perfume. After she was sworn in, she sat down and surveyed the hushed courtroom. Her eyes locked onto mine.

I stared at her ass, and she stared right back at me with this matter-of-fact-neck-twisting-eye-rolling look. She was purposely trying to intimidate me, but I was far from intimidated by her. And I damn sure wasn't gonna blink as I twisted my lips and stared at her hard enough to burn a hole into her soul.

Our noticeable stare-down was interrupted when the prosecutor began asking her a bunch of irrelevant questions one after the other. After ten more minutes of bullshit questions that were asked just so that the jury could get to know her a little bit better, the salt-and-pepper-haired male prosecutor pointed in my direction and asked Essence did she recognize me.

"Yes, I do," she answered.

"Can you tell the courtroom who she is?"

"I know her as Brazil," she answered, sounding very short and scripted.

"*Brazil*, is that her real name?"

"No, her real name is Marie Tavares, but myself and everyone that I know has always referred to her as Brazil."

"So is Brazil her nickname?"

"Yes, it is."

"Where did that nickname derive from?"

"Well, her father is of Brazilian descent and she used to travel back and forth to Brazil a lot, so that's where I always assumed the nickname came from. That was what I was introduced to her as, and that's just what I always called her."

"I understand," the prosecutor stated as he slowly nodded his head and paced the courtroom floor. "You said that she traveled a lot to Brazil. Do you know why? Was it for family or for business?"

"From the time I've known her, it was always for business."

I already knew where this was going.

"Explain what you mean that the trips to Brazil were for business."

"Well, like I mentioned earlier, I owned the gentleman's club in Queens and Brazil came to work for me as an exotic dancer. Like two weeks or so after she started working for me, she came to me and told me that if I put up ten thousand in cash that she could go back to her country and recruit ten women and bring them back to New York, where they could work in the club for me at a low rate. And she also told me that we could pimp them."

"'Pimp them'? What did you take her to mean by that?"

"Well, I took it to mean that we could have the Brazilian girls that she was gonna recruit come and dance in the club at low wages and at the same time we could offer them up as prostitutes," Essence said.

The prosecutor nodded his head. "Who came up with the prostitution scheme?"

"Brazil did. And she is the one who knew how to speak the same language as the Brazilian girls, so they were her responsibility, and she ran the entire prostitution operation."

The prosecutor then informed the judge and the jury of a particular number that referred to evidence that he wanted to introduce and then he focused his attention back on Essence.

"Listen really closely and tell me if you recognize the voices on this recording, as well as the premise of the conversation." The prosecutor pressed the play button on a CD player.

My voice said on the recording: *"Essence, them bitches ain't got no fuckin' choice. I control what the fuck they say, what the fuck they do, what the fuck they eat, and all of that shit, and if they asses ain't happy, then they gots to disappear. And, believe me, I'll handle the fuckin' shit the way I'm gonna handle it! It's about this paper."*

"Wow! Listen to your gangsta ass."

"I ain't bullshittin'. I'll stick a hot-ass curling iron in them bitches pussies before I put a fucking bullet in they heads and make all of them watch the shit! You feel me?"

The prosecutor stopped the CD player and then he asked Essence to explain to the jury what it was that they'd just heard.

Essence went on to explain to the jury that it was a conversation that she and I had in which I spoke to her about how I was planning on brutally and ruthlessly dealing with the Brazilian girls who complained about their jobs as strippers and whores.

"Did Brazil ever put a bullet in the heads of any of those Brazilian women like she claimed she would do?"

Essence paused and then she sighed for dramatic effect. "Yes, she did."

"Oh my fuckin' God!" I blurted out. "No, I didn't! Essence, how you gonna sit up there and just lie like that?"

My attorney tried to hush me.

The prosecutor objected, and the judge warned me to keep my mouth shut.

The hardest thing for me to do was sit there and listen to Essence repeatedly twist the truth and straight fabricate shit that she knew wasn't true. But there wasn't anything that I could do about it, and I just had to sit it out and wait until the next day when she would be crossed-examined by my attorney.

Essence had really gotten on my very last nerve. I was so heated, when we broke for lunch, I began snapping at my defense team, my relatives, and even some of my friends.

Vegas said to me as he approached me during the break, "The jury can see right through her ass. Don't worry about that shit, babe."

I stared at Vegas with a screw face and then I just barked on his ass and totally caught him off guard.

"What the fuck is this I hear about you fuckin' with that bitch Destiny?"

"What?"

"Vegas, don't play no games, just tell me the fuckin' truth, 'cause that bitch was talking real greasy. I just need to know if you was fuckin' with her or not."

"When did you speak to Destiny?"

"Don't worry about that shit! Just fuckin' answer me. And if you was fuckin' with her, please don't tell me you fucked her while Angie was wit'chu."

"You know what? I'ma just let this whole shit slide because I know you just real stressed out right now with this trial and all that."

Vegas was right. I was stressed out, and the fact that the nigga wasn't denying the shit made me know that Destiny had been telling the truth.

Right there in the courtroom I just started swinging on him, trying to beat the shit outta his ass. "How the hell you gonna disrespect me and our daughter like that, Vegas?" I shouted as I repeatedly punched him in his face.

Vegas didn't swing back, and luckily for him, the court officers rushed me and separated us.

My lawyer growled into my ear, "You're gonna blow this fucking trial. You gotta cool it."

"Okay, okay, just get off of me," I said to the court officers and my lawyer, as the judge and some of the jurors and the crowd of people looked on at what was going on.

I blew air outta my lungs and straightened my clothes and sat down and gathered myself. I was hoping that my lost temper hadn't just caused me to blow my trial.

"Be meek, baby. Just relax and be meek, you'll be all right." My grandmother leaned over the wooden bench and placed her hands on my shoulder.

"Okay, Nanna," I said as I placed my hand on top of her hand and nodded my head.

Chapter Thirty-seven

Essence

As soon as I made it into the bathroom stall of the courthouse I reached into my bra and I took out the vial of coke that I had stashed there. I quickly opened the bottle, poured the white powder onto my right hand, and began snorting it. Inhaling it is actually a better way to describe the feverish way that I abused the drug.

I had put on a perfect performance on the witness stand. But testifying against Brazil was one of the hardest things that I ever had to do in my life and I knew that I would have to be high in order to make it through the second half of my testimony and cross-examination.

I heard a female voice ask, "Essence, you in here?"

Immediately I froze. I didn't say anything and then I heard the bathroom door slam shut.

"Essence?" the voice asked again.

This time I heard the stall door next to me swing open.

"Essence, is that you in there?"

I could tell that whoever it was, they were standing directly in front of my stall.

"Yeah. Who's that?" I turned my face and the front of

my body away from the stall's entryway. I quickly snorted some more of my cocaine before putting the vial away and wiping my hands and face clean. "Yo, who is that?" I asked again.

"It's me."

"Who da fuck is *me*?"

"Essence, it's Kyra. Open up the fuckin' door."

Kyra was Chanel's little sister and she had been trying to get in touch with me ever since Chanel had been murdered at my house in Atlanta.

I unlocked the stall door and opened it and headed straight to wash my hands, not even acknowledging her.

"Essence, what the fuck is the deal?" Kyra asked me.

"Kyra, listen, I'm not in the mood for no bullshit, a'ight? I got a lot I'm dealing with right now and—"

"You dealing with a lot? Bitch, you a fuckin' snitch and you got my sister killed?"

At that point some white woman walked into the bathroom, and Kyra lowered her voice to that of an angry whisper. "Watch your back, Essence—That's all I'm gonna tell you—Watch your back." Kyra stared at me for a few seconds and then she walked outta the bathroom.

After I finished drying my hands, I exited the bathroom.

One of my bodyguards asked, "Everything a'ight?"

"Yeah, I'm good," I said before heading out of the court building to go get something to eat.

But as we exited the building, Kyra and some other chick that I had never seen before, along with three other thugged-out-looking dudes that I had also never seen before, seemed to be following us.

"We might have a problem with them right there," I said to my bodyguards as we walked down the steps of the courthouse and onto Queens Boulevard.

My bodyguards told me not to worry about it, and we kept walking and made our way into Applebee's.

Kyra and her crew finally did fall back and they stopped following us, but I was still on edge, so I immediately headed right for the bathroom when we entered Applebee's.

"I'm sorry, y'all, but my nerves are just on edge. I gotta go to the bathroom again," I said as I walked off.

Again, like a fiend I reached into my bra and I took out my cocaine and began snorting it. But this time I wasn't interrupted by anyone and I took my time getting high.

After about ten minutes the drug began to take effect and I started to feel nice and all of my fears, jitteriness, and inhibitions were slowly exiting from my body. I straightened myself up and cleaned myself off and headed back out into the restaurant.

"Y'all didn't order anything?" I asked my security. "Just order something, I got it."

I led them to the bar and we sat down. I ordered Buffalo wings and Hennessy on the rocks, and my security ordered chicken quesadillas and Sprite.

As soon as my drink arrived, I drank it in one shot and ordered another.

"Essence, you gotta take it easy," Kimani, one of my bodyguards, said to me.

"Yo, y'all don't know. I'm just dealing with a lot of shit right now. Shit that I can't even share with anybody." My head was really starting to feel nice. "I'm scared though. I mean, all my life I could just sense when some real serious shit was about to go down, and it's like I'm really sensing that something is about to go down," I said.

"What do you mean?" Kimani asked me.

My second drink arrived. I didn't drink that one as fast, but I did start to drink it. "I just think I'ma get caught slippin' and end up murdered. It's some scary shit."

"Essence, come on, you know we ain't gonna let shit happen to you."

"Y'all got me?" I asked with a big smile on my face. I was really starting to feel good from the liquor and cocaine running through my system.

"Gotcha," they replied.

I never even touched my wings, but I did have two more Hennessy on the rocks. By the time we made it back to the courthouse, I was tore up. But I maintained my composure, and although I was drunk, no one would have known.

I took the witness stand high as hell, but it helped me because I was so much looser. By the time it came for me to be cross-examined I was ready, and I did a fantastic job.

I blew a kiss to Brazil and sashayed past her after I'd finished my stint on the witness stand.

Brazil shook her head and looked at me, but she didn't say anything.

Kyra and her crew hadn't been in the courtroom in the morning, but they were there for the afternoon session, staring at me as I walked outta the courtroom.

I was still feeling high and was confident and ready for anything, so I stared right back at her. When I reached the row that she was sitting in, I stopped and motioned for her to come to me so that I didn't have to raise my voice.

When she made her way over to me, with my bodyguards flanking me, I smiled and then I whispered in her ear, "Fuck with me if you want to and your ass will end up dead just like your sister."

After I said that, Kyra pulled away from me. She didn't immediately say anything verbally, but I could clearly see the tension in her face as her jawbone clenched and she nodded her head.

"A'ight, it's on, bitch," she softly said.

I walked off with my bodyguards and made my way out of the courtroom and out of the courthouse and into a Lincoln town car that was waiting for us. Me and my two bodyguards piled into the car and made our way to Manhattan, where I was staying and hiding out at the Marriott Marquis hotel in Times Square.

When we reached the hotel, I went straight to my room and fixed myself a drink from the wet bar. Then I did two lines of cocaine before plopping down on my bed. I was depressed as all hell, but I was determined to stay in a constant fog from being high day in and day out.

You just put that bitch away, I said to myself as I thought about Brazil's impending conviction. *Yup, and she brought it on herself.*

Even with thoughts of having defeated Brazil I knew that I couldn't totally rest because I may have won that battle, but in doing so I had created a war. And now it was out there that I was a full-fledged snitch and there was a whole a legion of people who wanted to see me dead and who I knew would soon come gunning for me.

Chapter Thirty-eight

Brazil

The jury had my case in their hands and it was time to wait things out before hearing my fate. The unwritten rule was, if the jury took a long time in deliberations, then it was a bad sign for the defendant, but if the jury returned quickly with a verdict, then it was said to be a positive sign for the defense.

Well, only an hour into jury deliberations, the District Attorney approached me and my lawyer and offered us a deal where they were willing to drop the RICO charge against me and I would get sentenced to just seven years in prison, provided that I pleaded guilty to the conspiracy charge.

"Brazil, you gotta take that," my lawyer said to me, a bunch of eagerness in his voice. "No one knows how the jury will decide. They had a strong witness testifying against you, and the bottom line is that if you get convicted you're looking at twenty-five years to life. That versus seven years."

My mind was resolute. I knew I wasn't taking shit. I couldn't believe how soft my attorney was. "Fuck that! I ain't taking no deal. Before the trial they didn't wanna talk to us because Essence had flipped and they had her as their ace in the hole. Now that the trial is over, they're coming to us trying to make a deal? Get the fuck outta here! They doing that shit because they nervous that the case ain't gonna go their way. That's the only reason they coming at us like this."

My lawyer frowned his face up and ran his hand across his brow. "I don't know, Brazil, I just don't know if you're making the right decision."

I remained resolute, and we relayed our intentions back to the shocked District Attorney.

As it turned out, the jury deliberated for that entire first day without reaching a verdict, and I would be lying if I said that I didn't think twice about that deal as time went on. But halfway during the second day of deliberations the jury notified the judge that they had reached a verdict.

We had hung around the courtroom, so when we were notified we immediately made our way into the courtroom. My heart was pounding, and my mouth was dry from the second that I walked into the courtroom.

It took close to an hour for all of the pertinent people involved in my case to arrive, but eventually everyone who needed to be there was there. Vegas was there, my grandmother was there, my mom was there, and a whole bunch of my friends were there. My daughter wasn't there, but that was because I'd made it clear that I didn't want her to be in the courtroom on the day that the verdict came in, simply because if the verdict didn't go my way, I didn't want the image of me being carted off in handcuffs to be the last image she had of me.

The defense was asked to stand up.

I blew air out of my lungs and I stood up alongside my lawyer, my hands folded behind my back. I thought about closing my eyes and praying, but at the end of the day I knew that praying at that point wasn't gonna change anything because the verdict was already set.

I stared at the jury and tried to figure out if I could read their minds, but none of the jury members would look me in the face.

"Jury foreman, please step forward," the judge instructed.

I clinched my teeth and held my breath. I had to hold my breath because I didn't want to appear nervous, but the fact is, I was terrified and I felt like I was about to pass out.

"Has the jury reached a verdict?" the judge asked.

"Yes, Your Honor, we have," the tall dark-skin Michael Jordan look-alike juror stated.

My lawyer reached over and patted me on my leg in an attempt to show his confidence in me.

I was still holding my breath. I felt like I was gonna die with anticipation. Then I heard the words, "We the jury find the above titled defendant—"

Those were the last words that I remember hearing because, before the foreman could finish saying what he was saying, the courtroom had erupted with cheers from my supporters.

"I told you, baby!" Vegas shouted.

I heard my grandmother thanking Jesus.

The judge banged his gavel, trying to restore order in the courtroom.

My lawyer was smothering me with his tight embrace. "You beat 'em," he said to me and then kissed me on the cheek.

"Did he say *not guilty*?" I asked for confirmation.

"Yes! You beat all the charges," he cheerfully replied.

After the judge was finally able to restore order, he conversed back and forth with the jury foreman. Then he thanked the jury for their diligent service and released them. The judge spoke to me and my lawyer, and he wished me well.

"Thank you," I said to him. I more mouthed my words than I spoke them, but I knew that he'd got the point of how grateful I was.

Then my family and friends swamped me with hugs and kisses.

"You did it, Essence! You did it!" Vegas hollered.

My grandmother couldn't stop praising the Lord.

"Grandma, don't cry," I said to her as I wiped her tears away. She was gonna make me start crying, but I knew that I had to be strong and maintain a confident image to whoever might be watching.

As we began to make our way out of the courtroom, all I could think about was holding my daughter. I couldn't wait to see her.

"Essence, hi. I'm Karen Wilshire from the New York *Daily News*. Do you mind if I ask you a few questions?" the reporter asked me.

"I really don't have the time. I just wanna go see my daughter," I told the reporter.

"Can you just tell me how you feel?" She stuck a small tape recorder in my face.

I smiled. "I feel like I just won the lotto!" I kept walking out of the courthouse with my entourage, and the reporter kept right in tow.

"One last question, actually is there anything you'd like to say?" she asked me.

I kept walking and I thought about what she had just asked me. Then I thought about who she was and how she had the power to give my words a voice, so I stopped. My entourage stopped with me.

"Yeah, I do wanna say something. I want everybody to know, especially my daughter, that I am the last of a dying

breed. They don't make muthafuckas like me no more—
Excuse my French, Grandma," I said to my grandmother
and the reporter before continuing on. "What everybody
seen during the course of my trial was they seen me stand
the fuck up and face the heat, while everybody around me
copped out, took deals, snitched, and all that kind of shit.
Everybody rolled over on me, but I stood up like a woman
and I took my case to trial and I won. I been shot up, rail-
roaded and all of that, and I'm still standing! I'm still here!
What! It's a beautiful thing. I'm a beautiful woman, and my
intergrity can NEVER be questioned, and make sure you
print that for all the snitches and cowards to read."

Somebody from the crowd shouted, "Preach!"

"Can we get a picture of you?" the reporter asked.

"Most definitely," I replied. "Make sure you get the
heels in that shot. These are eight-hundred-dollar shoes
that I'm rocking right here. We can't leave that out." I
posed like a supermodel for the reporter's photographer.

After we were done with the photos, we all piled into
waiting SUVs and headed home.

"We partying tonight!" I screamed out loud. I asked my
homegirl for her cell phone, so I could start calling everybody that I knew and telling them to come to my grandmother's house.

As I dialed numbers, I told Vegas that I wanted him to
break out the barbecue grill and to call one of the local
deejays and have them come over to my grandmother's
crib so we could get things poppin'. It was a Friday, so I
figured, what better day than a Friday to party and celebrate my trial victory, and that was just what I was gonna
do.

So as all of my people began making preparations for
my victory party, I had two pressing things that I had to
handle. The first was making it over to Angie's school so
that I could surprise her by picking her up.

Angie got out of camp at two forty in the afternoon, and it was close to two thirty when I arrived with my grand-mother. Her camp was at her school. At first I was gonna lay in the backseat of my grandmother's car and wait until she got close to the car and then surprise her, but instead I decided to wait right at the front door of the school so that she would see me as soon as she came out.

At two forty kids started to emerge from the school with their teachers, and after about five minutes, I saw Angie walk out of the school with one of her little friends. She was so busy running her mouth with some little girl that she didn't even see me or her grandmother.

"Excuse me, little Ms. Lady." I had a huge smile on my face.

"Mommy!" Angie yelled. She dropped her book bag and came charging toward me. "I didn't know you were com-ing to pick me up." Angie hugged me and held on to my neck as if she was holding on for dear life.

"I wanted to surprise you. And guess what? I'm gonna be able to pick you up every day from now on!" I said to her.

And those were the best words that I could have ever imagined hearing myself say. I knew how fortunate I was, because the next time I picked up Angie from school could have easily been when she was graduating from college.

"You promise?"

"I pinky-promise," I said to Angie as we brought our pinkies together.

We started to walk off to my grandmother's car. A few of the other parents remembered who I was from the time that I had been shot by Destiny right near Angie's school, so they came up to me to say hello and to ask me how I was doing, and to make small talk. When we were done with the small talk, we went to the car and headed back home.

Angie knew exactly how to manipulate me, but she was so cute and I had missed her so much that no matter what she asked me for, at that moment I would have given it to her. She was able to persuade me to take her to Carvel for ice cream and then to Toys "R" Us, and after leaving Toys "R" Us she had me take her to McDonald's.

I literally had no money, but my grandmother looked out for me and slid me fifty dollars and told me not to worry about it. So Angie was happy, and I was ecstatic. But I still had something else that I wanted to handle.

As soon as we got home I reached inside Angie's book bag. I took a piece of paper from her notebook, grabbed a pen off of my grandmother's table, and made my way to the bathroom. I locked the bathroom door, grabbed a magazine to rest the piece of paper on, and I began writing a response letter to Destiny.

Dear Destiny:

By the time you read this letter, I'm sure that you will have heard that I beat ALL of the charges! That's right, a bitch is a free woman. I know that probably brings tears to your eyes, but that's the difference between me and you. I'm a real chick and you're not. I'm a free woman and you're not.

Yeah, you might of fucked my man, and that's all good. Actually, I should ask you, was the dick good to you? I'm sure it was, but I can promise you that if you could trade in fucking Vegas, if it would mean your freedom, that you would do that in a heartbeat. But you can't regain your freedom, and the reason your ass is locked up is because all of the foul shit that you did over the years finally caught up with yo' ass.

I ain't gonna be long-winded. I got real shit to do, like party and drink and celebrate beating those charges. Did I tell you that I'm a free woman? Oh yeah, I think I did tell you that already. My bad, LOL.

 But anyway, I'll do like you said and I'll kiss Angie for you. It feels so good chillin' with her, you don't even know. I'm sure you're doing good with all those prison walls to look at and all that prison food to eat. If you do happen to get depressed, just think about all the money we could of made and all the moves we were about to make, and how you threw all that shit out the window when you decided to side with that snake, Essence. Now look at the both of y'all. Both of y'all asses are pitiful.

 I'll holla!

One

Brazil

P.S. "Hate it or love it the underdog is on top and I'm gon' shine until my heart stops!"

I folded up the letter and placed it in an envelope to mail off later after retrieving Destiny's address.

When I was done with that, I was off to get drunk and high as a kite so that I could party my ass off and live up what I almost missed out on for a quarter century.

Chapter Thirty-nine

Essence

It had been three weeks since Brazil had beaten her case. And, I have to admit, the fact that she had gotten off was eating at me to no end. I was still feeling depressed from the whole HIV thing and was continuing to medicate my feelings by drinking and getting high.

I had been back and forth between Atlanta and New York, and while I was constantly watching my back due to the haters and the people who still had gripes with me, I was also plotting and planning to get at Brazil.

The word on the street that had came back to me was that Brazil had made up her mind that she was gonna get out of the whole strip club and party scene altogether. Supposedly she was gonna be heading back to college during the upcoming semester to study law and she wanted no distractions. I'd also heard that she had become lovey-dovey with some dude named Mitch who worked as a repairman for Verizon. It got to the point where I felt like I was becoming obsessed with her. I had to know her every move.

I knew that the best way to find out what was up with

her was to track what was up with her daughter. So what I did was, I went by Angie's school at eight o'clock in the morning and waited for her to arrive for camp.

Sure enough, at about eight thirty, Angie and her mom pulled up to the school in a black 525 BMW that was driven by some light-skinned pretty-boy dude with curly hair. He had to be the Verizon dude that she was so in love with.

I thought about approaching Brazil right there on the street, just to test her and see what was up with her, but that would have been stupid. Instead, I pulled off and headed to this town in Queens called Cambria Heights, where I was renting a house, since I had already sold my house in Bayside.

When I reached home I scanned my brain trying to remember the phone number for this supervisor who I knew that worked at Verizon. Her name was Shellie Wilson and I had gone to high school with her. Me and Shellie had been cool in high school, but after high school we lost contact. But we would run into each other in the street or at the mall, and each time we saw each other, we would exchange numbers. But with all of the moving that I had been doing, and switching cell phones and all of that, I'd lost Shellie's number. So I started calling all of the people who I was still cool with who might know her, and still I had no luck in tracking down the phone number.

I decided to just call Verizon's main corporate number and see if I could track Shellie down that way, and sure enough the corporate operator at Verizon was able to bring up a number for Shellie. She didn't give me the number, but she was able to transfer me to Shellie's extension.

"This is Ms. Wilson. How can I help you?"

"Shellie?" I asked, wanting to make sure that it was her who had picked up the phone.

"Yes, this is Shellie. Who's calling?"

"Hey, Shellie, this is Essence," I said with a smile.

"Oh, what's up, girl?" Shellie sounded very excited to be hearing from me.

"I couldn't begin to tell you the half."

"Yeah, I been hearing through the grapevine—"

I quickly cut Shellie off, to set the record straight "Don't believe any of them rumors you hearing about me, because there's a lot of haters out there. But, listen, I need a favor from you."

"Okay. What's up?"

"I'm adding another line in my crib and I don't wanna wait forever. I was hoping that you could pull some strings and get somebody to come out to my house today," I explained.

Shellie told me that she didn't work in the area that governed the repairmen but that she could make some phone calls and pull some strings for me.

"You still in Bayside?" she asked.

"Nah, I sold that crib and bought something down in Atlanta, but I'm staying in Cambria Heights now, on 234th Street." I went on to give her my full address.

Shellie took all of my contact information and told me that she would call me back in a few minutes.

"Listen, Shellie, I need one more really big favor, if you can do it. I know that I'm asking for a lot, but there's this repairman named Mitch, and I met him the other day. I don't know his last name, but he is a cutie! I was wondering if you could possibly get him to come out to my crib to install the new line."

Shellie began laughing into the phone. "Girl, you are too much. So this is what this is about?"

I laughed and told her that I really did need the other line installed.

She laughed and said in a playful and sarcastic way, *"Yeah, okay.* It depends where this Mitch guy works out of. Like if he works in Brooklyn or in the Bronx, then I won't be able to get him to come out, but if he works out of a garage near Cambria Heights then I should be able to make it work. I got pull up in this company," Shellie explained.

"Okay, so call me back and let me know. And me and you keep saying we gonna hook up and hang out but we never make it happen. We really need to hang out and get some drinks or something," I said.

"No doubt, we gotta do that," she said before we ended the call.

I went about my day and started making myself some breakfast and trying to figure out exactly what I was gonna get into for that day.

After I ate breakfast I took a shower. Before I could finish drying off from my shower, my cell phone was ringing. It was a call from the 212 area code.

"Hello?" I said as I picked up the phone naked and dripping wet.

"Essence?"

"Yeah, it's me."

"You paying for the first and second rounds of drinks when we go out. Mitch will be at your crib before twelve noon," Shellie said to me.

I smiled and thanked her. I told her that I would pay for all the rounds of drinks. All she had to do was let me know when she wanted to hang out.

"He don't even work out of the garage that covers Cambria Heights, but I told his supervisor that it was a job for my sister and that I specifically wanted him to handle it. It worked out because he doesn't work too far out of that district."

"That's why I called you," I said. "Thank you, sweetie."

"Anytime," Shellie replied. "I'll call you sometime next week and we'll definitely hang out."

"Okay."

I was happy as hell and I was also a little nervous because I was hoping that I would be able to pull off my plan. I quickly finished drying off and then I applied baby oil all over my naked body. I rummaged through my clothes, looking for the sexiest outfit that I could find. I wanted to wear something that would entice Mitch and instantly get his dick rock-hard.

I found some boy shorts and a matching tube top and I thought about putting that on. And then it hit me that I should just stay naked and wrap only a towel around me. I had a pink fluffy terry cloth towel that stopped just below the start of my butt cheeks and extended to just above my titties. I looked at myself in the mirror. With my baby-oiled skin I was turning myself on, so I knew that I looked good.

At about eleven thirty my doorbell rang. I looked out the window and saw a Verizon truck parked across the street from where I was staying. I quickly walked to the front door and opened it.

"Hello. I'm here to put in a new phone line for Rachel Wright?" Mitch said to me. He was referring to my real name, which he must have got from his handheld computer.

"Yeah, that's me. Come in, come in," I said. "I just got out of the shower. I didn't expect you to come by until twelve," I explained with a smile.

Mitch nodded his head. He looked at me and squinted his eyes as if he was trying to figure out who I was.

"Is something wrong?" I asked, trying to break the trance he'd slipped into.

"Oh no, nah, um, so where do you want this new line installed?"

"Upstairs. Come on, I'll show you." I led Mitch upstairs to my bedroom. I made sure to walk in front of him so he could see my ass as I walked up the steps.

"I'm gonna put a desk right over there, so I want the line right in that corner. It's gonna be for my computer."

Mitch went and looked at where I had pointed to, and then he looked to see where my current phone jack was at.

"So how long you been working for Verizon?"

"Too long," Mitch joked.

Then there was a moment of awkward silence followed by him saying that he had to run outside to his truck for a minute.

When he left, I thought about what I should do. I knew that I just had to be straightforward and direct with him, so as soon as he returned back upstairs, I set my plan in motion.

"So how long do you think this will take you?" I asked.

"Oh, about twenty minutes and I should be done."

"You want something to drink? Water, juice, a beer?"

Mitch respectfully declined.

"You mind if I get dressed in here while you work?" I asked him.

Mitch turned and looked at me, and I immediately dropped my towel.

He smiled and chuckled as he stared at my body. "Nah, I don't mind that at all," he said and continued on with what he was doing.

I paraded around my room butt-ass naked, and I was looking in my closet and in my dresser, pretending I was really looking for something to put on. Finally I put on my boy shorts underwear and my tube top and then I laid on my stomach and stretched myself across my bed.

"So what do you do?" Mitch asked me.

I smiled but I didn't say anything.

"Something wrong?"

"No," I replied.

I could tell that I was making him feel a little uncomfortable, so I spoke up. "Can I just ask you something?

And I know this may be from left field somewhere, but I just wanna know," I said.

"Yeah. What?"

"You go into different houses every day, and I'm sure you meet nice pretty women. I'm just curious—Have you ever fucked any of the customers that you meet? Because I think shit would be so hot and off-the-hook if you did." I stared at him.

"Wow! I wasn't expecting that. Actually I've met people on the job and then hooked up with them later, but actually doing it on the job, nah, I never did that before."

I wasted no time. I stood up and walked over to Mitch. I asked him to stand up, since he had been crouched down in the corner working on the phone jack. He stood up and was much taller than me, so I stood up on my tippy-toes and whispered into his ear, "I am so horny." I then grabbed his hand and guided it toward my pussy.

Mitch followed my lead and began rubbing on my clit. His big strong hands felt good on my clit.

I started to moan, but it wasn't about me and my enjoyment, it was about me fucking Mitch raw so that he could bring back "the monster" to Brazil. I wanted to see her try and survive and beat HIV, since she seemed to have nine lives.

So that Mitch wouldn't punk out and change his mind, I quickly unzipped his pants and pulled out his dick. He was definitely working with a little something, but I was able to deep-throat his entire dick, and I could tell that he was loving it.

"You want me to stop?" I stroked his dick and looked up at him from my kneeling position.

"Hell no. Suck that shit, baby."

I made sure his dick was nice and hard and then I un-buttoned his pants. I pulled them down to his ankles. His tool belt and all of his tools hit the floor, leaving him standing there with an erect dick and in only his work boots. I quickly stood up and, without asking for his permission, I turned around and guided his dick into my pussy

As Mitch started fucking me doggy-style, I screamed and moaned and hollered. From the way he was pumping his dick, he seemed like he was a two-minute brother. I know I was making him feel like a porno star, but I didn't want him to cum just yet.

I turned around and said to him, "Fuck me in my ass." I wasn't a big fan of anal sex because to me the shit hurt like hell. But I knew that since Mitch was fucking me raw, there was a better chance of him getting the disease from me if he fucked me in my ass, simply because I always bled just a little bit every time I did have anal sex.

Mitch was slow with the instructions, so I slid his dick out of my pussy and guided it toward my asshole.

"Woo yeah, right there, but be easy, baby," I said, coaching him. "Oh God! Your dick is so damn huge!" I lied, all to boost his ego.

Mitch's dick was now fully in my ass, and he began to slowly work it. I was in pain, but I knew that it would be over soon and my mission would be accomplished. I rubbed on my clit to help medicate the painful thrusts that I was receiving.

Thankfully, after about two more minutes, Mitch was getting ready to cum.

"Oh yeah, baby, I'm gonna cum!" he hollered.

I was gonna tell him to pull out, but I wanted him inside of me because every second counted, in terms of him getting "the monster." Or at least that's what I reasoned. "Uggghh!" Ugggh!" I yelled as he came inside of my ass.

"Was that good?" I asked as he rested his body on top of mine and breathed heavily.

"Hell yeah, that shit was off the chain," he said. He finally pulled out of me and started to fix his pants and adjust his tool belt.

While I lay on my bed, I got some tissue and tried to push his cum out of my ass.

"That shit looks sexy like a cream pie," Mitch said to me.

"You like it?" I asked. "I hope that means that I'm gonna see you again, right?"

"Definitely. I gotta give you my digits so we can have round two later on."

"You know, don't even worry about that other phone line." I explained to him that it would be a waste because I was gonna be heading out of town soon.

"You sure?" he asked.

"Yeah, I'm sure. I gotta head back to Atlanta. I was just up here taking care of some loose ends."

Mitch gathered his things, and he and I exchanged cell phone numbers. He told me that he was running behind schedule and that he had to go.

As soon as he walked out of my door and made it to his truck, I called his name and waved for him to come talk to me for a quick second.

He got out of his truck and kept it running and he trotted over to me. "What's up?" he asked.

"Nothing much. Just do me this favor and tell Brazil that *Essence* said she is so fuckin' lucky to have your ass, okay? And make sure you tell her how you put that dick on me today, okay?"

Mitch instantly turned bloodshot-red, and his face frowned up. All he could say was, "Get the fuck outta here."

"I'll talk to you later," I said. "Make sure you relay that message for me though," I added, before closing the front door. *Now go home to your little bitch*, I thought to myself.

Chapter Forty

Destiny

I was in the middle of working on my book when my mail arrived. I wasn't surprised to see that I had a letter addressed from Brazil. I'd heard that she had beaten her trial, so I knew that it was just gonna be a matter of time before she came at me boasting. When I opened her letter and read it, I saw all of the slick jabs that she was trying to take at me.

I quickly took a break from writing my book just so I could get all up in Brazil's ass. I was sick of her shit and it was time to set her ass straight. I needed to let her know that even when I lost, I was a winner.

Brazil,

Yo, so I got your little letter and the first thing I did after I read it was smile. And I'll admit that I was definitely hatin' on you from the sidelines. You did your thing and you beat your case. Good for you. I was certain that you was gonna blow trial, but you didn't. I was wrong. I been wrong before, and I'll be wrong again.

But is it just me, or were you trying to boast and throw slick little jabs at me in your letter? Like this slick comment that you made when you said: "I'm sure you're doing good with all those prison walls to look at and all that prison food to eat."

And that other slick comment that you made at the end of your letter when you said: "Hate it or love it, the underdog is on top, and I'm gon' shine until my heart stops!"

Really, though, right from the beginning of your letter, you started off talking real greasy when you said: "I'm a real chick and you're not. I'm a free woman and you're not."

Brazil, matter of fact, BITCH—that's what I'll refer to you as from now on, a BITCH—because that's all you are, nothing more nothing less. Now, BITCH, this is what you need to understand. You need to know that even when I lose I win. What exactly do I mean by that? Well, I thought that you would be smart enough to figure out what I was trying to tell you in my letter to you. But apparently you're not the brightest light bulb, so I'll spell out for you now so that we can be clear.

BITCH, I have HIV. Yes, you read that right and you can read it again, and I'll say it again—I have HIV. You know that virus that causes AIDS? Yeah, well, I have that virus. I fucked your baby's daddy Vegas. In fact we fucked raw-dog every time we fucked, never even thought about using a condom. Now how many times has Vegas fucked you after he fucked me? Good question. But only you can answer that.

So, Brazil—I mean BITCH—when was the last time you got tested for HIV? Why don't you go get tested and after you get the results from that test let

me know what it feels like to be a free woman who's walking around with a death sentence?
I NEVER lose! You BITCH!

> *Crystal Jackson*
> *a.k.a.*
> *Destiny*

P.S. Stop interrupting me and let me finish this future best-seller that I'm working on.

Chapter Forty-one

Brazil

God had truly been blessing me. Since the end of my trial I had applied and been accepted to John Jay College of Criminal Justice. I was so excited. I had always wanted to go to college, but I had gotten addicted to fast money that I earned from stripping and all of those plans for college went out the window. But now I was more focused than ever, and with everything that had gone down with me and with all that I had learned about the legal process, I knew that I wanted to be a lawyer. Law was starting to intrigue me like I never imagined anything school-related could. I was planning on becoming a criminal lawyer because I felt that I could be the most passionate in that particular area.

In addition to my plans for college, I was also starting to really fall in love with this dude name Mitch. Mitch was one of the first "regular" dudes that I had ever messed with. I say regular because he wasn't a thug, he wasn't a hustler, and he wasn't an aspiring rapper or artist or someone connected to the music industry. Mitch worked for Verizon as a repairman and he was a regular nine-to-five type of dude. He wasn't a square or anything like that. He drove a BMW, he had his own crib in the Canarsie section of Brooklyn. He had no kids, and he looked good as hell. Actually Mitch was the perfect catch. But what's funny is, he was exactly the type of guy who in the past I wouldn't have given a chance to holler at me and get to know me.

Thankfully though I had given Mitch the time of day when he had saw me walking one day and he pulled over in his Verizon truck to talk to me.

"Excuse me, miss, can I talk to you for a second?" Mitch had asked me that day.

I smiled at him to not be disrespectful and I told him, "I'm sorry, but I'm really in a hurry," I said, trying to make it inside of Chase Bank before they closed at three.

I had kept walking and I made it into the bank. I was on line when Mitch walked in and got on line behind me.

"Can you at least tell me your name?" he asked me.

I had jumped because he startled me. It was like he had appeared from out of nowhere.

"You scared me," I laughed and said. "My name is Brazil."

"Really? That's a pretty name. Just as pretty as your smile."

"Thank you." I looked at Mitch and that was when I was able to see just how fine he was.

"I know it seems like I'm stalking you or something, but I never approach women like this. It's just something about you and I had to say something to you, and if I didn't, I would have been kicking myself later," Mitch explained.

"Is that right?"

"So, Brazil, are you married?"

"No," I said with a smile.

"You got a man?"

"No, I don't." I continued to smile.

"So then would you mind giving me your number and letting me call you later, and maybe we could go hang out and get some ice cream or something?"

"Ice cream?" I asked.

"Yeah, it'll be off the hook, trust me," Mitch said to me.

"Nah, you gotta come better than that," I said as I moved up in the bank line. "I mean, you ain't even tell me your name and here you are asking me for my number and telling me you wanna take me out for ice cream?"

"Oh, my bad. My name is Mitch."

"Okay, so now we're getting somewhere. Mitch, I like to eat and I like to laugh. So if I give you my number we can hang out, but we gotta go somewhere to eat and somewhere to laugh. Either a funny movie or a comedy club, you feel me?" I said.

"Oh, no doubt. You can call the shots, ma," he said.

I was gonna be called next, so I asked Mitch did he have a pen and a piece of paper so that I could give him my number. He took out his cell phone and put my number in his phone. And that was how we met. We had ended up going out with each other the next day, and then the day after that, and the day after that.

It was like I had become addicted to Mitch. I couldn't get enough of him. And I was with him at every free moment that he and I had. I had told him all about my past and he accepted it and he still wanted to rock with me. He loved Angie, and Angie thought that he was the funniest person alive, and they interacted so well together.

I didn't wanna scare Mitch and start talking about marriage or anything serious like that, but I really felt like he could be the one that I would eventually settle down with. I knew I had to take things slow, but he was just so perfect. Even the sex with him was off the chain. He knew how to cook. He wasn't a momma's boy. He was just perfect. He even told me that he was willing to help me out financially while I went to school so that I wouldn't have to try to work and go to school. I just couldn't believe how good Mitch was to me, and he and I hadn't even been messing with each other for that long. So I had no choice but to believe him when he would tell me that from the moment he saw me that it was love at first sight.

So as I was basking in my new relationship and making plans for my bright future and trying to put my past behind me I was also subconsciously wondering just when something was gonna go wrong. It was like things were going just way too smooth and too good for me.

Destiny had written me a letter, and I purposely hadn't opened it. I sat on it for weeks because I didn't wanna deal with the negative energy that I knew she was gonna come at me with in the letter. In fact, I don't know why I even held on to the letter because everything inside of me was telling me to just throw the shit out. But I held on to it, and I have to admit that part of me was curious to know what she thought and felt about my freedom.

I decided to open the letter and I began reading it. And as I read it, my heart rate picked up and I started to breathe really heavy.

Brazil, this bitch is lying, I said to myself.

I then re-read her letter just to make sure that I had read it correctly.

HIV, I thought to myself.

I immediately got angry, but I was too scared to remain angry for long. I began exhaling air from my lungs and I tried my best to calm myself down. I told myself that Destiny was bullshitting and was only trying to get my pressure up.

She just wants the upper hand, I told myself. *But what if she ain't lying?* I had to ask myself that question. "Oh my God!" I screamed out loud and I wondered just how could someone be so heartless and ruthless. "Uggggghhhhhhh!" I screamed. Thankfully no one was home with me at the time.

I began thinking about all of the times that Vegas and I had had unprotected sex and I wanted to kick myself for being so stupid and for having trusted that stupid mutha-fucka. But what really began to eat at me was the fact that I had broken all of my rules with Mitch and I was having unprotected sex with him too so soon! The last thing that I would have wanted was to have passed anything on to Mitch. That would have hurt me more than me actually being HIV-positive.

All kinds of thoughts began running through my mind. But the most pressing thought of all was that of my daughter. Immediately I thought about my death and what would Angie do without me.

I felt like I was gonna go crazy. I knew that the only way for me to find out if Destiny was lying or not would be for me to take an HIV test and find out for sure. But going to take that test was easier said than done. I had no idea how I was gonna come up with the courage to actually take the test and then get the results. I didn't know how I was gonna do that. But I knew that I had to find out my status.

I plopped my body down on my bed and I thought about how profound Destiny's words could be. I was defi-nitely a free woman, but the question was, was I just a free woman who was walking around with a death sen-tence?

Chapter Forty-two

Essence

Part of the reason that I was constantly back and forth between New York and Atlanta was because Sean Coleman and I were having our secret sexual rendezvous, and since Sean had to be in New York, it made sense that I came to New York instead of having him travel all the way down to Atlanta.

Sean was the former city councilman who had helped me broker my deal with the district attorney that had guaranteed my freedom and subsequently landed Shabazz in jail and almost landed Brazil in jail.

Sean was no longer in the City Council, he had since moved on to bigger and better things. He was now the mayor of New York City. An election that he had won partly due to the fact that he had exposed police corruption based on the whole Shabazz thing. Sean and I had stayed in contact with each other ever since I had contacted him, but now that he was the mayor, his every move was scrutinized. He had to watch everything he did and everyone he associated with. So he and

I would always see each other after hours at a neutral spot like a hotel, or somewhere safe and out of the public's eye.

The hotel thing had started to get tired, and that was one of the reasons why I decided to start to renting this house in Cambria Heights. I wanted Sean and I to have a more warm and homey type place to chill at and that was exactly what we had in my Cambria Heights spot.

I had long knew that Sean was dying to get in my pants, and I finally gave him the chance to fuck me about two weeks after he had became mayor. Part of me let him fuck me just due to the fact of who he was. He was a powerful black politician, and it made me feel good to know that I was the one that he was digging. But on the flip side, Sean turned out to have a possessed penis. It had to be possessed because every time he fucked me he had me screaming and speaking in tongues, bringing orgasms outta me that I never knew were possible.

I couldn't believe that I had been turning him down for all of those years that I had known him. But it was all good because all it meant was that we had a hell of a lot of sexing to do to catch up on what I had been missing out on.

Sean would always come through to see me at like two in the morning. He would have his driver drop him off at my place and we would chill for like five or ten minutes, smoke some weed and drink liquor, and then we would fuck each other's brains out for two hours. The routine was always the same, and it never got boring.

After we were done fucking, we would take a shower together, and then at five in the morning I would drive Sean back to City Hall in my car so that he could get started on his day. I would then head to the gym and get

my workout on before heading back home to eat breakfast and sleep.

"I just wanna stay here and sex you for like the next
twelve hours," Sean said to me as we lay in my bed.

"So let's do that. Just call your deputy mayor and let
him know that you won't be available today."

"I wish it were that easy," Sean said me as he got up and
made his way to my bathroom.

I didn't take a shower. Instead I tried to be different. I
ran off to the kitchen and cooked some breakfast that
Sean could eat on the way back to City Hall. He would always have me stop at Dunkin' Donuts so he could purchase that bland processed food, and I just felt like
making him something that was home-cooked for a
change.

I quickly whipped up some grits, sausages, and eggs,
and I put it in a Tupperware bowl and I covered the bowl
with one of those snap-on lids so that the food would stay
warm. By the time Sean had finished showering I had already cooked his food and had thrown on my workout
gear and sneakers.

"You cooked this for me?" he asked.

"Yeah, I just figured that you had to be getting tired of
them tired-ass processed eggs and bagels from Dunkin'
Donuts." I poured Sean some coffee into a coffee mug.

The sun wasn't even up as Sean and I departed from my
house and approached my car.

"I still want you to stop and get the newspaper for me,"
Sean said as he looked so fucking good in his suit. He hadn't
put on his tie yet, and that was because he usually changed
his clothes altogether when he got to City Hall.

"Okay, I gotta get gas anyway," I said to him as I deacti-
vated my car's alarm.

Sean got in the front passenger's seat, and I got in the
driver's seat. "I put cheese in your grits. I don't even know

if you like 'em like that," I said to Sean as I stuck the key into the ignition.

"What? I love cheese—" Unfortunately Sean's words got cut off, and he never got to finish that sentence.

In fact he and I never even made it to City Hall.

Chapter Forty-three

Destiny

I couldn't believe what I was seeing as my face became glued to the television. Some of the other inmates had come running to find me and they rushed me into the TV room to take a look at what had transpired earlier that day in Queens.

I looked at the television and listened as the news anchorwoman said, " 'The Promiscuous Girl' killed after her car explodes this morning in an apparent assassination. Good afternoon, I'm Lori Stevens and we begin today with a story that has rocked New York City. Police are trying to confirm if New York City Mayor Sean Coleman was inside of a vehicle that exploded this morning in the quiet middle-class section of Queens known as Cambria Heights. Many are saying that the vehicle's explosion is reminiscent of a Mafia-style gangland rubout. And if Mayor Coleman was in that vehicle, there are a ton of questions that everyone will be asking. Was this a professional hit on the New York City Mayor, or was Rachel Wright the target of the hit? Rachel Wright, who goes by the name of Essence, and is the former infamous owner of the Promiscuous

Girl nightclub. Some of you may recall, she was a key witness in the NYPD corruption case that involved a highly
decorated NYPD detective with a high-ranking father in
the police department. We're gonna go live to our reporter,
Rick Nolan, who is live at the scene and who'll help us sort
out some of the details. Rick, what do you have for us?"

I quickly ran to the phones to start calling some of my
people and everyone that I spoke to confirmed that shit
was definitely real. Essence was up outta here. She was
dead.

Part of me was sad knowing that we had had so much
history together. But I think a bigger part of me was sad
because I hadn't gotten the personal satisfaction of beating her. I wanted to be the one who had taken her out, or
at least I wanted to be the brains behind her subsequent
death.

What could I do? I had to live with the hand that I was
dealt. And with Essence out of the picture, it meant that
there was one bitch down and one to go.

Chapter Forty-four

Brazil

I had finally gotten the courage to go to the doctor and take an HIV test. As it turned out, taking the test was the easy part. The hard part was waiting the two excruciating and nerve-wracking weeks for the results. I had decided not to say anything to Mitch, or anyone else for that matter, until I knew for sure what was what.

During those two weeks, I had become the most religious person in the world. I went to church two Sundays in a row, and I prayed three times a day. I even opened up the Bible and read from it every day. God probably was able to see straight through me, but I didn't care. I pleaded and bargained with Him every day, hoping to influence the results of my test.

Finally the moment of truth had arrived and the day was here when I was supposed to go in for my test results. That morning I was so nervous that I couldn't eat anything. I was constantly going to the bathroom from the moment that I had woken up. My cell phone also would not stop ringing, but I didn't answer it. I wasn't in the mood to speak to anyone.

But at around nine thirty that morning I got a text message on my cell phone from one of my homegirls named Fatima that said: *Brazil, you heard what happened to Essence? That bitch got killed! Can you believe that shit?*

Without hesitation I dialed Fatima.

"Girl, what the hell are you talking about?" I asked.

"Brazil, where you been? That shit is all over the news! Essence and Mayor Coleman both were in Essence's car and that shit blew up. The news is saying that it was definitely a hit."

"Wow! That is crazy." I grabbed my remote control and turned on the television to this all-day cable news channel called New York 1.

Fatima was still talking, but I was paying her no mind as I focused my attention on what the news was saying.

"All that foul underhanded shit that she did over the years finally came back to her ass! I knew it would. I knew it!" I screamed out in excitement.

Fatima was in agreement with me. We spoke for about a minute more. I told her that I had to go because there were a ton of other people that I wanted to talk to.

I hung up the phone and I watched the news some more. I have to say that there was not one ounce of me that felt the least bit sorry for Essence. As far as I was concerned she had gotten exactly what she deserved, and I looked at it as just one less headache that I had to worry about.

What was weird was that as I watched the news and listened to the radio and spoke to my true friends, it was like I felt like this heavy burden just lifted off of me. Destiny was in prison and locked away for years, and now Essence was dead. I had outlasted the both of them. I had won!

I was really feeling amped and charged. I figured that it was no better time to go to my doctor and learn my test results firsthand. In a weird way, Essence's death had given me a lot of confidence. I was certain that the results would be negative. It was the last battle in the war, and I needed to fight it and just get it over with.

When I arrived at the doctor's office and told the receptionist who I was and what I was there for, she told me to have a seat and that the doctor would be with me in about five minutes. My palms were extremely sweaty as I waited, and although I was confident, I still clutched a picture of my daughter, which was attached to my key chain.

"Marie Tavares, the doctor will see you now." A nurse held open the door for me that led to the doctor's private office.

"Hello, Ms. Tavares. Have a seat," the doctor said to me.

I came in and sat down in front of his desk. I refused to look the doctor in the face, and my heart wouldn't stop beating.

"So I have the results to your test," the doctor said.

I looked up at him, and it was as if things were going in slow motion. I saw the doctor remove the eyeglasses that he was wearing. He pinched the bridge of his nose, while squinting his eyes.

"Please tell me everything is okay," I said to him.

"Ms. Tavares, I'm afraid I can't tell you that. Unfortunately your test came back positive. You have HIV."

"What?" I said in disbelief and despair. I buried my face into my hands. I felt like I was gonna faint. All of a sudden I heard this loud ringing sound and I opened my eyes and the room appeared to be spinning around as if I was dizzy.

"Please tell me that there's some kind of mistake, please!" I begged the doctor as tears began to fall from my eyes.

The doctor frowned his face and slowly shook his head. I could tell that he was looking for the right words to say.

"Ms. Tavares, I wish I could tell you that there was

some kind of a mistake, but these tests are pretty accurate. Of course we will do a re-test but barring a miracle—"

"Why? Why me?" I cried out loud as I cut the doctor off in the middle of what he was saying.

There was no need for me to wave the white flag in surrender because I had clearly been defeated and I had no idea how I would continue on. I was devastated.

Chapter Forty-five

Essence

"I didn't know that shit was gonna be that loud and that powerful," I said to Jason as I quickly hopped into the rented Toyota Camry that he was sitting in parked at the end of my block. I was out of breath after having run the length of my entire block to get to him.

"That's that C-4 military shit. We had two of them joints! That shit ain't no joke, right?" Jason hastily backed up the car, and we peeled off.

Jason had already explained to me well in advance that he was gonna use a remote control device to detonate the explosives that were to be attached to my car hours before the explosion. The hardest part in me carrying out the car bombing plot had been my ability to trust that Jason wouldn't detonate the bombs until after I had gotten back out of the car.

See, Jason had been cool with Shabazz for years and therefore he and I had also been cool. But the last time that I had spoken to him was probably around the time that King Tut had punked Shabazz. And right after that time everything had went downhill with me and Shabazz, so there really had been no reason for me to have spoken to Jason.

Needless to say I was shocked as all hell when Jason had showed up at my crib in Cambria Heights. He didn't come at me on no rah-rah nonsense and had totally come in peace. Jason was straight-up with me when he told me that Shabazz wanted my ass dead and that he had counted on him to carry out my murder.

"Jason, why the fuck are you really here?" I asked with a bit of an attitude.

Jason told me that he could have easily not knocked on my door and just plotted to murk me. "But, see," he added, "I ain't do that shit. I'm here out of respect, Essence. We go back and we got history, and it's time for all of this bull-shit to end. And I'll keep it real with you. That shit that happened down in Atlanta, that was me behind that shit. You wasn't supposed to live, but you did. Shabazz is flip-pin' out and he wants you dead. Now there's two ways we can handle this. You can tell me to get the fuck outta here and I can bounce and leave and you can stay watching your back. Or you can hear me out and let me lay down to you how we can end this shit where you get what you want, I get what I want, and Shabazz gets what he wants," Jason explained.

Me and Jason continued to speak for about fifteen more minutes, and since he was straight-up with me about being behind what had happened in Atlanta, I fig-ured that he didn't have any ulterior motives. So I decided to go through with what he was proposing.

Basically, Shabazz wanted me to die in a car bomb as-sassination plot. And to prove it, Jason played a copy of a recording of Shabazz that he managed to get when he had visited him in prison.

"Yeah, she staying at this crib in Cambria Heights," was what a voice that sounded like Jason's said, as he played back the recording.

"Jason, that's right around the way. You gotta move on her ass now. And don't fuck that shit up like them niggas did that you sent to Atlanta. I want you to personally handle this, a'ight?"

"That's Shabazz right there," Jason spoke quickly and explained to me. I listened as closely as I could, trying to confirm that it indeed was Shabazz.

"If all of her shit is in ATL, then what is she driving in New York?" the voice that sounded like Shabazz's asked.

"I ain't even sure," Jason responded.

"Jason, you sleeping on the job, my nigga. Find out what she pushing and rig that shit Mafia-style."

There was a pause as the tape continued to play but no one spoke.

"Come on, I know you ain't bitchin' up on me now." Shabazz blew out a lot of air from his lungs in disgust.

"Nah, I'm just saying, maybe we should let this shit cool down and die some more and then hit that chick as soon as she gets comfortable."

"Jason, the bitch is already comfortable! She back in New York and she got a million enemies right now. So what that says to me is that she don't give a fuck and she's just thumbing her nose at everybody. And if you think about it, now would be the perfect time to hit her ass, because there would be a bunch of possible suspects that would want her dead right now since everybody knows that she's a rat. If we let that shit die down, then it won't look right if we were to move on her later on."

Again the tape continued to roll, but there were no audible voices.

"Yo, Jason, you was there with me when we took out King Tut, and if you think that bitch won't roll over on your ass, you are fucking crazy. She probably talking to the cops right now!"

"You shoulda never told her about that shit."

I heard the sound of someone sucking their teeth, and then I heard what sounded like someone banging their fist on a table. Then I heard more silence.

Shabazz said, *"But she knows and that's the bottom line,"* before the tape went quiet again.

Meanwhile my mouth dropped open in shock because I had just found out with certainty what had actually happened to Tut. And if that was Shabazz on the tape, I immediately knew that he had lied to Jason and told Jason that he had informed me about Tut's murder when he in fact hadn't.

"My nigga, listen to me. Go to Howard Beach and get that shit from them white boys and then find out what she pushing and rig that muthafucka. She'll get in, start that shit up, and—BOOM!— her ass will be up outta here."

"I'll make it happen," Jason replied.

"You got me on this, right?"

There was a pause and more silence.

"I gotchu," Jason answered.

The tape stopped, and then Jason looked at me.

"So that was definitely Shabazz?" I asked, sounding uncertain.

"Yes," Jason emphasized as he pressed rewind. He played a segment of the tape one more time, just to hammer it home for me.

"Jason, you sleeping on the job, my nigga. Find out what she pushing and rig that shit Mafia-style."

"Tell me you hear that nigga's voice," Jason said.

"Yeah, it's him." I blew air from my lungs. I desperately

felt like I needed some weed or something to ease my nerves. "So how did you get that tape?"

"Essence, I'm a fuckin' New York City cop! You think a prison guard is gonna question me? I can walk up in a prison with whatever."

After stating that, Jason went on to explain that he had to let Shabazz believe that he was going to go through with this plan because he still felt extremely vulnerable. Vulnerable in that he had in fact helped Shabazz kill King Tut, and he knew that at anytime either me or Shabazz could have looked to make things better for ourselves by trying to pin the King Tut murder on him.

"Wow!" I ran my hand down the front of my face.

Thankfully for me, Jason had had a change of heart about assassinating me. But what he had devised was a way that I could die without actually dying.

"You got my word that I won't detonate that shit until you get out of the car and step away from that shit. And as soon as you do, you have to haul ass the other way because the explosion is gonna be powerful," he'd explained to me.

"A'ight, I got that. But what I'm saying is, when it's all said and done, won't my bones or my teeth or something have to be in the car or at least nearby? And if not, then how suspicious would that look?" I asked.

"I already got that covered." Jason explained that he would have the skeleton of this old female snitch informant who had been killed and buried in a Brooklyn backyard.

"Her bones will be your bones, and we can have that shit in the backseat covered up or we can put it in the trunk. Won't nobody know the difference because, after that shit explodes and the fire that follows, trust me, nothing will be all that identifiable."

I nodded my head and I told Jason that I would trust him on it, but I still wanted to know why. "Why, Jason? Why would you put yourself at risk like this just to help me?"

"Essence, you see where Shabazz is at? He's there because he didn't know when to say when. And I know when to say when. After this shit, I'm done with all of the games and the underhanded shit. So if you with it, you with it, and we'll both be on the hook for this. And if we can both be on the hook, then I know you won't ever say shit, and neither will I. And, like I said before, we'll both be getting what we want."

Jason was right, and I knew that I would feel bad about Mayor Coleman, but what the fuck could I do? I was with the Jason's plan. I knew that it was my only alternative to end all of the beef and to cease all of the people who wanted to see me dead for being a rat. Although I was really only gonna be dead "on paper," as far as everyone else would be concerned, I would be physically dead, since no one would know what me and Jason knew.

Early that morning as I cooked breakfast for Mayor Coleman, I knew that I could have won an Academy Award for the way that I acted so smoothly and didn't even let on in the least bit as to what was about to go down.

"*I put cheese in your grits. I don't even know if you like 'em like that.*"

"*What? I love cheese—*"

"Oh shit, Sean, hold up. I forgot my ID card for the gym," I said, cutting him off in the middle of his sentence. "Let me run inside and get it. I'll be right back."

After saying that I stepped out of my car and instead of heading back in the direction toward my house, I bolted and headed toward the end of my block. And the next thing I heard was two of the loudest booms that I had ever heard in my life.

"Holy shit!" I said after turning and seeing the huge fireball that was once a car burning in front of my house.

Glass from some of the surrounding cars and homes shattered, and multiple car alarms were set off due to the explosion.

"Essence, you got my word, I ain't saying shit and don't you ever say shit to anybody," Jason said to me as he pulled up next to his car and got out of the rental, which he let me take.

"Jason, don't worry. I'ma burn this shit when I get to where I'm going and I'ma be good." I quickly exited the passenger side of the car and briskly walked around to the driver's side, hopped in and pulled off.

Jason went his way and I went mine. And just like that, the war was over. And as far as I was concerned, I had won.

But if I had to be honest with myself, I knew that there were never any winners in wars, only losers. Both sides in any conflict suffer losses. I had suffered losses, Brazil had suffered losses, and Destiny had suffered losses. So the question boiled down to not who won the most, but rather, who lost the least. And again, that was me.

NOW AVAILABLE

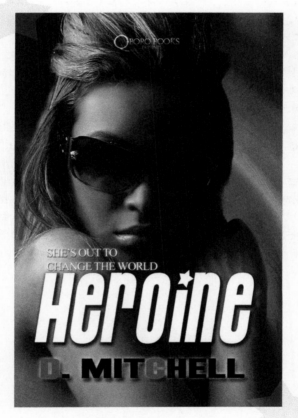

The baddest woman in town is not a gangster girl or a ride-or-die chick. She's a third generation assassin who has plans to change the world.

MORE TITLES FROM

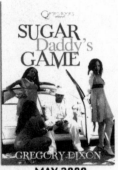
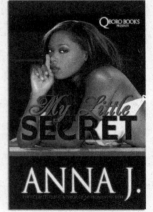

AVAILABLE
DECEMBER 2008

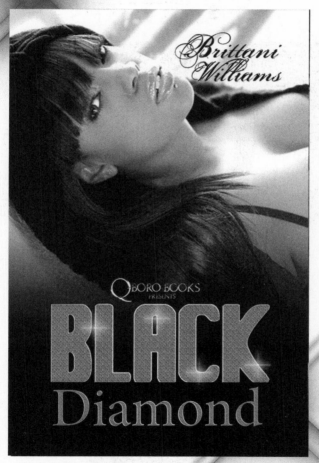

Black Diamond proves why some details are meant to be kept secret. The result of simple pillow talk will leave two best friends fighting to survive.